A Lassiter's Christmas

A Gems and Gents Novel

Copyright © 2014 by Iris Bolling
All rights reserved.

No part of this book may be reproduced in any form or by any electronic or mechanical means including information storage and retrieval systems, without permission in writing from the author. The only exception is by a reviewer, who may quote short excerpts in a review.

Printed in the United States of America
ISBN: 978-0-9913426-5-5

This is a work of fiction. Names, characters, places and incidents are with the product of the author's imagination or are used fictitiously, and any resemblance to actual persons, living or dead, business establishments, events, locales is entirely coincidental.

SIRI ENTERPRISES
RICHMOND, VIRGINIA
www.sirient.com

www.irisbolling.net

Books By Iris Bolling
The Heart Series

Once You've Touched The Heart
The Heart of Him
Look Into My Heart
A Heart Divided
A Lost Heart
The Heart

Night of Seduction Series

Night of Seduction/Heaven's Gate
The Pendleton Rule

Gems and Gents Series

Teach Me
The Book of Joshua I – Trust
The Book of Joshua II – Believe
A Lassiter's Christmas

Brooks Family Values Series

Sinergy
Fatal Mistake
Propensity For Love

Table of Contents

Chapter 1

Chapter 2

Chapter 3

Chapter 4

Chapter 5

Chapter 6

Chapter 7

Chapter 8

Chapter 9

Chapter 10

Chapter 11

Chapter 12

Epilogue

Books by Iris Bolling

Chapter 1

The siren from the ambulance could be heard as it pulled up to the bay with another gunshot victim. It was number four in the last twelve hours. The signal of the door swooshing open sounded as he stripped the soiled gloves from his hands and dropped them into the waste bin. He ran his hands under the hot water washing them as thoroughly as he could before the nurse slipped another pair onto his hands.

"Two entry wounds, one exited, one lodged near the spine," the EMT stated, as they pulled the gurney from the back of the vehicle and rushed through the double doors. "Massive blood loss. Believed internal bleeding." The portable monitor beeped indicating the victim's heart had stopped.

Dr. Theodore Prentiss jumped onto the gurney and began chest compressions. His white coat swung wildly behind him as attendees pushed the gurney quickly down the corridor towards the trauma room.

Four hours later, an exhausted Theo, as his friends called him, exited the operating room, in a clean pair of scrubs, a book bag over his shoulder and weary over the fact that he had only saved three lives from reckless violence. None were over the age of eighteen, yet they had no problem taking another person's life. At their age, he was thinking about college, girls, girls and college. Not guns, turf, or drugs. What in the hell is the world coming to? He wondered as he walked past the nurse's station.

"Goodnight, Theo," one nurse, with blonde hair and blue eyes called out.

Theo stopped and turned just as the head nurse, Mrs. Gordon, rounded the corner. "He is Dr. Prentiss to you, Amber." She looked at the young nurse sideways. "Don't let me correct you again." She then looked up at him. "Goodnight, Dr. Prentiss." She nodded with a slick smile and a wink that Amber could not see.

"Good night, Nurse Gordon, Nurse Hayward." He nodded, smiled, and then turned to walk out of the emergency room door exit. He understood what Nurse Gordon was doing. There was never a time when any of the nurses would call other doctors by their first name, for all the others were either foreigners or of the Caucasian persuasion. However, he was an exception. He understood his position and accepted it for what it was. He was the number one trauma surgeon in the area; he was thirty years old, unmarried and an African American male. He wasn't supposed to be in the position he was in, but hell, God put him there, along with his parents who worked long, hard hours to see him reach this point.

The cold air hit him the moment the doors opened, then swished closed behind him. When he came in seventy-two hours ago, it was nice, so he hadn't bothered to wear a coat. Yes, it was the weekend after Thanksgiving, but in Virginia, the weather varied from the high 50's to the low 30's. All he wore in was long johns under his scrubs and his timberland boots. Now he had to walk in the cold from the ER to his vehicle that was parked on the lowest level of the hospital garage. On top of that, somewhere along the way it had snowed.

Theo quickened his pace as he walked down the ramp leading to the lowest level of the parking garage. It was a little past two in the morning and all he wanted to do was climb into his king-size bed, with his thousand count sheets, temperature controlled room, and the hot meal he had just set his microwave to cook from his tablet. The next forty-eight hours were his to do with as he pleased. And it pleased him to just sleep. No drama, no suspense and definitely no gunshot wounds. Only one thing was missing from his thoughts as his vehicle came into sight and that was a woman between those sheets with him. "Yes, that would clinch it," he said as he looked up.

A noise captured his attention. His steps slowed as he took a quick glance around the parking lot. It was empty. He pulled his keys from his pocket, then hit the button to unlock his vehicle. Looking behind him again, still nothing, but he heard a voice, mumbling. He opened the door with the intent of getting in and going home, but there was the sound of distress in the voice. If the person was injured and he didn't at least attempt to help, he would never forgive himself. He placed his book bag in the passenger seat, then closed the door. Slowly, he walked around one of the cement pillars in the parking lot and froze. He closed his eyes for a few seconds, then opened them again to make certain he wasn't dreaming.

The hood of a car was up with the loveliest round bottom he had ever seen bending under it. Long legs clad in black leather boots, extended beneath a short black skirt with thick thighs. The voice was a little clearer. The woman was cursing up a storm at the vehicle. The trunk of the vehicle was up and the driver's door was wide open. On the ground he saw a purse, with what appeared to be all the contents of said purse at her feet and a crowbar.

He stopped, took a moment to evaluate the situation. They were at least seven floors below the entrance to the hospital, in an underground garage, with no one around and a crazy woman was beating up a vehicle.

Ouch, he thought as she missed the tire and kicked the rim. He heard her curse as she bent down to grab her injured toe. The woman fell against the car grimacing in pain.

He slowly approached the woman. "May I help you with something?"

The woman quickly bent down, picked up a device from the ground, then turned pointing it at him. For a second he jumped back thinking it was a gun and he was about to become a victim like the ones he had just saved. He threw his hands up.

"Hey, hey, watch where you wave that thing."

"Where in the hell did you come from?" The woman looked around, surprised at his appearance.

"The hospital." Theo pointed to the building. "Where did you come from?" he asked in a slow assessing voice.

"From the hospital."

"Were you just released?" He chose his words very carefully.

"No, I was visiting my brother's..." She waved her thought away. "What do you want?"

What a natural beauty, he thought as she stood there in a short black leather jacket, with her short skirt, knee high boots, and afro with a band pulling it away from her face. No make-up, just tearstains running down her cheeks, from the most expressive brown eyes he had ever looked into. "Just thought you may need some help?"

"Well, I don't." She gave him a sideways sister girl look and attitude.

It was two in the morning. He had worked three straight days. Attitude was not something he wanted to deal with regardless of how fine a package it came in. "Not a problem." He threw up his hands then turned.

"Just like a man to walk away," the woman huffed under her breath.

Theo stopped, turned back about to respond when he saw her pick up the crowbar and began beating on something under the hood of the car. The sight was so adorable he stood there smiling. He could walk away —hell probably should walk away, but there was no way he could leave her out here this time of night alone. Suddenly, she stood with the crowbar in her hand and was about to strike the windshield of the vehicle from frustration. He ran over, grabbed her around the waist, picking her up off her feet, and shook the crowbar from her hand. The metal hit the cement with a clamor just as the heel of her boot connected with his jewels, causing him to buckle to the ground. His grip on her never loosened and she landed right on top of him.

She attempted to scramble up, but he held her firmly.

"Stop it, damn it," he spoke calmly, but clearly in pain. "Breaking the windshield of the car is not going to make it start. Now stay still." He tightened his hold on her.

"Let me go," the woman demanded, just before he caught the elbow she was about to land in his throat.

He wrapped his arms around hers, then threw his leg over hers to keep her from kicking him again. "Calm down. I'm just trying to help you."

"You can help me by letting me go." She threw her head back, but collided with this stubborn chest rather than his nose as she intended.

"Stop fighting me."

"What in the hell did you expect, coming up behind a sister like that. You're lucky I didn't hit you with the crowbar."

"You're lucky I haven't lost my temper yet. Now be still," he demanded. Taking a moment to get himself under control, he slowly began to untangle their bodies. Not one to trust what the woman would do next, he held her down with one hand as he stood. He then extended his hand down to help her up. The angry brown eyes were hesitant. Then she reached up and took his hand. They stood there assessing each other for a long moment. Neither was oblivious to the appreciative glare being shared.

"My car won't start." She was the first to speak up.

"Really," and raised a sarcastic eyebrow. "I thought you just liked hanging out in a parking lots inciting brothers."

She smiled, and to his surprise, dimples appeared on the dark smooth skin.

"That's my day job." She turned towards the car. "You know anything about cars?"

"No. I have this thing called a mechanic I call whenever I have problems with a vehicle."

She looked over her shoulder at him. "Figures." Then bent back under the hood.

"Why don't you lock up the car, I'll take you home and call someone about the car in the morning."

The woman turned back towards him. Looked him up and down. "You work here?"

"Yes," he replied.

"What's your name?" she asked as if assessing if he was trustworthy.

"Theodore Prentiss and yours?"

She hesitated, then extended her hand. "Pearl Lassiter."

"Well, Pearl Lassiter. Let's lock up, grab your things and get out of the cold."

Pearl nodded, thinking, baby, it may be cold outside, but inside, her body was at lava point from the tangling of their bodies. However, she began picking up her things from the ground and placing them back inside her purse. This was not a booty call moment. She was tired, frustrated and still upset about her brother.

Theo closed the trunk and the hood of the car. He stood next to the door as she gathered her things. "Do you need anything else out of here?"

Pearl shook her head. "No. I'll get it in the morning." She looked around, but didn't see any cars. "Where are you parked?"

He tilted his head. "Behind the pillar," he replied. He held out his hand. "Let's go."

Pearl hesitated for a moment, then walked in the direction he pointed. He placed his hand on the small of her back as if it was the most natural thing in the world. They walked down the short ramp to his vehicle. Pearl stopped, looked at him, then looked at the vehicle again. "What kind of work do you do at the hospital?"

"I help people," he replied. "What kind of work do you do?" he asked as he opened the passenger door to his G-Class Mercedes SUV, for her.

"I talk to people," she replied as she stopped, took a picture of his license plate with her phone, then sent it to someone. "Just in case you're a serial killer or something. My family will know how to find you."

He closed the door as she got inside, trying hard not to react to the thunder thighs she displayed under her skirt. Once inside, he pushed the button to start the vehicle. "If I really wanted to harm you, I could do it here, throw your body into the woods behind the parking deck and no one would be the wiser until your body began to deteriorate and dispense an odor."

He had the nerve to smile at her when he said that. "It sounds like you have thought about that possibility a little too much."

Pulling out of the parking space, he grinned. "Just once or twice. Where to?"

She gave him the address, then sighed as the warmth of the heated seats began to set in. "So you know, I have six brothers and five sisters who will hunt you down like an animal if you do anything to me."

"You mean like, save you from a bad situation in an abandoned parking garage and taking you home at two in the morning out of the cold, snowy night."

"Yes, something like that." She grinned and looked out of the window.

Theo smiled as he looked in both directions before pulling out of the garage. After driving for a few minutes, he asked, "Did you say something about your brother being in the hospital?"

"Yes, he's visiting with his woman," she husked.

The way she said the word woman, then rolled her eyes and looked out of the window made Theo chuckle. "I take it you don't like her."

"No, I don't like her. She's one of those light bright women with the long curly hair and hazel eyes who thinks every man in the world is supposed to bow at her feet just because."

"Don't hold back your feelings," he laughed. "I want you to tell me what you really think of her."

Pearl glared at him across the interior of the vehicle. That was the second time tonight he had made her smile. He glanced at her and smirked.

"Sorry." She looked out of the window. "It's been a rough day."

Outside, snow began to fall lightly, coating the city skyline with its lights glistening in the background. The building with twenty or more floors would leave lights on inside offices to spell out *Happy Holidays*. Inside, where the atmosphere should have been a little strained for two strangers, it had fallen into a comfortable silence. When they reached the turn for interstate 64 or 95, the GPS system told him to go straight. He hesitated.

Pearl looked over at him. "Is something wrong?"

"No," he replied. "I've never been to this part of town before."

"Are you from Richmond?"

"No, Chesterfield."

Pearl laughed. "Oh, you're a suburbanite."

"You say that as if it's a bad thing."

"You say no…Chesterfield, as if Richmond is a bad thing."

Theo shook his head. "I don't know if it's good or bad. I've never lived in Richmond."

"You work at the hospital, that's Richmond. Don't you go out to eat or explore downtown?"

"I'm running from the moment my feet hit the floor, until I leave. I rarely get to sleep or eat when I'm there. And why are you making me feel as if I have to defend living in Chesterfield?"

"Maybe because of your hesitation to go across the bridge back there," she huffed. "Why don't you pull over? I can walk from here."

"I'm not going to drop you off to walk in the snow. Nor am I going to have this ridiculous conversation because I don't live in Richmond," he hissed. "This is what I get for trying to help a sister out."

"Look, I didn't ask for your help."

"I gave it anyway. The least you can do is be grateful." The GPS system indicated they had reached their destination. Theo pulled the vehicle over and parked in front of a two-story home with a wraparound porch, nice big yard and a vehicle parked in the driveway. Another vehicle pulled around them, and stopped in the driveway as he stepped out. He walked around to open the door for her.

"Where do you think you're going?"

"I'm walking you to the door, as a man should do late at night."

"It's not like we were on a date or anything. You just gave me a ride home. That's all."

"Are you combative about everything or is it just me?"

Hands on her hips, she took offense. "I'm not combative."

"You could have fooled the hell out of me."

"Is there a problem here?"

Theo turned to see a tall, tall, tall, dark-skinned man standing behind him.

"No, Daddy, there's no problem. Mr. Prentiss was just leaving."

Theo extended his hand, looking up at the man he estimated to be a good seven feet tall. He was six-two and had to look up at the man. "How do you do, Mr. Lassiter? There is no problem. I was explaining to your daughter how a man should treat a woman, even if she doesn't act like a lady." He gave her a stern look.

Pearl looked appalled. "How dare you. You don't know me like that. In fact, you don't know me at all."

Joe Lassiter looked from his daughter to the man she was arguing with, then looked around. "Pearl, where's your car?"

"At the hospital," the two answered angrily.

Joe raised an eyebrow. "Why is it still at the hospital?"

"It wouldn't start. I'm going in the house," she announced then stomped off.

"The ungrateful little wench," Theo murmured, as he looked angrily away from the house.

Joe stood there staring from his daughter, who was now at the door of his house, then back at the man who didn't seem as if he planned on leaving. "Would you like to come in for some coffee, Dr. Prentiss?"

Theo looked up wondering how he knew he was a doctor. Joe pointed. "The label on your scrubs, the tag hanging from the mirror in your car, added to the murderous look in your eyes you are trying to fight. The Hippocratic oath will get you every time if you hang around Pearl long enough."

"Sir, I just met your daughter less than an hour ago, and I don't mean to insult you, but your daughter is a bit on the…. bitchy side. I'm not calling her out of her name. It's the only verb I can think of to describe her at this moment."

Joe, with his easy way, patted Theo on the shoulder. "Why don't you come in, have a cup of coffee and tell me what's going on with Pearl's car?"

"Thank you, sir, but it's been a long night."

"It wasn't a suggestion, son," Joe stated as he gently guided the man into the house.

Chapter 2

The moment he stepped inside he felt at home. The door opened to a long hallway that led straight to the kitchen, which seemed to be the hub of the house. It was the wee hours of the morning so Theo didn't expect anyone to be up and about, but he was wrong. They passed the living room on the left, a few feet down was a staircase with garland wrapped around the bannister with a huge red bow in the center. On the right was a family room, with three large sofas and two recliners at the top of the oval shaped room. Inside the room was a decorated Christmas tree in the corner. In the center was a brick fireplace with stockings hanging around the huge mantel. Above each stocking was a silver-framed picture. In the center was a huge picture of what appeared to be a family. A large flat screen television was above the fireplace. The room was warm and inviting. He could imagine watching football games in that room. Further down the hallway was a huge kitchen, which he saw from the doorway. From there he could see it connected to a large dining room and an enclosed side porch.

Theo followed Joe into the room, where he greeted a petite woman with deep dimples, and a short haircut with a seductive mixture of grey. Theo stood in the doorway as the couple kissed, not once considering curtailing their hello because a stranger was in the house.

Joe finally came up for air and turned to him. "Dr. Prentiss, my wife, Sally. Sally, this is Pearl's friend Dr. Prentiss."

Sally extended her hand. "Friend, you say." She smiled. "That's not exactly how Pearl described you a moment ago, but welcome." Sally pointed to the table. "Please, have a seat."

"It's Theo. I don't want to interfere," Theo stated. "I've pulled a long shift and if it's all the same to you, I'd like to get some rest."

"But I just made a fresh pot of coffee and cobbler for my husband." Sally placed the cobbler on the table. Steam was rising from the center filling the kitchen with its wonderful aroma. "Surely you have five minutes to spare."

His mouth was watering the moment the cobbler hit the table. "I may be able to spare a few minutes," he said as he pulled out a chair.

Sally smiled, then winked at Joe, who sat at the other end of the table. She had just poured a cup of coffee and placed it in front of Theo when Pearl appeared. She had changed clothes to a pair of sweats, a midriff top and slippers. "Why do you have your feet under my table?"

"Last I heard it was my table," Joe said as he filled his mouth with cobbler. He looked up at Theo. "What do you think?"

"Heaven," Theo replied as he ignored Pearl.

"Daddy, aren't you supposed to be at work?" she huffed.

"My husband came home to have his lunch break with me. One day if you change your attitude you may have a husband to do the same for you." Sally sipped her coffee, then took a seat at the table.

Pearl started to speak, but Joe beat her to it. "I only have an hour for lunch, Pearl. I don't want to spend it hearing you degrade men. Now, have a seat and tell me what happened to your car."

Pearl slumped into the seat across from her mother as she poured her a cup of coffee and smiled at Theo. She thanked her mother then proceeded to tell her about the car and why she was at the hospital.

"Well, I'm happy to hear you are giving Samuel and Cynthia your support. You can't help who you fall in love with."

"That's true." Joe nodded. "Besides, it wasn't Cynthia who was in a relationship with you. It was that dumb jock. He's the one who stepped out. You really shouldn't be upset with her."

"And it was so long ago, Pearl," Sally added. "You really need to move on."

Pearl looked at them, appalled. "I can't believe you are discussing my business in front of a stranger."

"Dr. Prentiss is not a stranger," Sally replied. "The moment he helped you and brought you home, that made him family."

Theo looked up from the cobbler and smiled. "Family," he chuckled.

"So you're a doctor now?" Pearl screeched. "What other lies have you told my parents?"

"Don't disrespect your parents' table by raising your voice," Theo scolded.

Sally and Joe glanced at each other and grinned, quickly lowering their heads so Pearl wouldn't see it.

"I'm not disrespecting my parents," she said a little calmer. "You are by telling them you're a doctor."

"What's all the yelling about?" Phire, the sixteen-year-old daughter of the Lassiter's, asked with sleepy eyes. She sat on a stool at the breakfast bar.

"Sorry we woke you," Sally said to her daughter. "Phire, this is Pearl's friend Theo. Theo, our youngest daughter, Sapphire, we call her Phire."

Phire stood up and shook Theo's hand. "Hello, Dr. Prentiss."

"Hello, Phire," Theo replied just as Pearl cut him off.

"Why are you calling him doctor?"

Phire looked at her as if she had lost her mind. "Has she been drinking?" she asked her parents who shook their heads. She looked back at Pearl. "His scrubs have Dr. Prentiss on the front."

Theo smiled and turned to her. "See." He ran a finger across the name. "Dr. Prentiss."

"You didn't say you were a doctor."

"You didn't ask."

"I asked if you worked at the hospital."

Theo replied coolly, "And I replied yes."

"But you…" He cut her off by putting a forkful of cobbler in her mouth.

Phire laughed. "Finally, somebody found a way to shut her up." She stretched. "I'm going back to bed." She kissed her mother's and father's cheeks. "Night, Pearl." She waved. "See you next time, Dr. Prentiss."

"There isn't going to be a next time," Pearl announced.

Phire looked at her and smirked. "Sure there will." She waved her sister off and left the room.

Theo stood. "I'll have my mechanic tow your car to the garage. He'll take a look to see what's causing the problem."

"We have a mechanic," Pearl lied.

"Who?" Joe and Sally asked in unison.

Pearl gave them a look.

Theo smiled. "Mr. and Mrs. Lassiter, thank you for the cobbler and coffee." He rubbed his stomach. "I know I'm going to sleep well tonight."

"Thank you for assisting Pearl." Joe shook his hand.

"Yes, thank you for bringing her home," Sally added. "Pearl, show Dr. Prentiss out."

"With pleasure." She quickly walked out of the room.

Theo took his time. "Goodnight," he said then joined Pearl in the hallway.

She stood with her hands on her hips and the front door wide open.

Theo stopped in front of her five-four frame and wondered aloud, "Do you have problems with all men or is it just me?"

"I don't have a problem with men."

He smiled. "Then I'm going to take it as a compliment that it's me. I get to you, don't I?"

"Mr. Prentiss, or whatever you call yourself, I don't like arrogant, elitist suburbanites who drive a hundred thousand dollar automobile and look down on people who live on the wrong side of town. Being in the same room with them makes me sick to my stomach."

What gives her the right to judge him? The only thing he did was stop to help her. Yes, he hesitated before turning in the neighborhood. It was an area he had never visited before. He had no idea if he was in Richmond, Henrico or wherever. Did he deserve the bashing she was dishing out? Hell no, then it dawned on him. The lady protests a little too much. Before thinking, he pinned her against the wall, wedged his thigh between her legs to keep her from inflicting any damage to his jewels, held her hands above her head, and kissed her with a voracity he had never experienced. The intent was to make her eat her words, but that mouth of hers was so sweet, he had to savor the taste a little longer. It was provocative, the way he devoured her mouth, not caring that they were in her parents' hallway, with the door wide open and the cold air filtering in. When he felt her vigorous response, he stroked her tongue over and over again until he couldn't take any more.

He pulled away, liking the look of her kiss swollen lips, the look of tenacity on her face, but most of all, the loss of those stinging words that seemed to spill so easily from her lips. Her eyes fluttered open. Disbelief and confusion was there. He gave her his card.

"Call me in the morning. I'll prescribe something for your upset stomach." He turned and walked out of the house without looking back.

From the staircase above, Phire laughed. "That was hot. The doc's got moves." She stood and disappeared down the hallway.

Pearl looked around to see her mother and father standing in the kitchen doorway.

"Daddy, did you see what he did?"

"Yeah, I saw. You want to close that door. You're letting the heat out."

"The heat walked out with Dr. Prentiss." Sally smiled then walked away.

Pearl stood there in the hallway alone. *What in the hell just happened?* Every nerve ending was pumping exuberantly through her body. Her lower lips were moist; no, they were wet as if she had just had an orgasm, which wasn't possible from a kiss. *Or was it?*

From the moment she'd looked up and saw the tall fine man standing there she felt a tingle deep down in the bottom of her stomach. When he tackled her and placed his thigh over her legs, she wanted to spread them wider. His arms generated warmth like a blanket, and his breath on her neck felt like a smooth caress. No man had ever made her feel like that. It was her who set the boundaries with men. She liked getting her freak on as much as anyone else, but she also liked having control. This man took that away from her and she didn't like it. Didn't like it one bit.

Chapter 3

This was right. It felt so right it bordered on sinful, but Theodore didn't care, he wanted the sensation of her body next to his to continue. His mind did not register the sound of the telephone ringing for it was consumed with joy from this woman's touch. He kissed her neck, her shoulder, the swell of her breast and was right at the tip of her nipple when that irritating sound of the phone rang out again. This time the woman pulled away. He grabbed for her, but she was out of his reach. He sprang up in bed, hard as steel. Sweat was streaming down his chest, as if he was in a sauna. He wiped his hand down his face to find he was drenched there as well.

"What in the hell?"

The phone rang again. He grabbed his cell, pushing the button without looking. "What?"

A voice on the other end gasped. "That is not the proper way to answer a telephone, Theodore. What if it was the hospital calling? You must watch your tone at all times."

Theo fell backwards onto his pillows. "Mother," he sighed. "What could you possibly want this time of morning?"

"It is well after seven, Theodore. You should be on the golf course with your father and Dr. Pritchard."

Theo loved his mother, he truly did. However, there were moments, such as this, when he could literally choke her to death.

"It snowed last night, and I worked a seventy-two hour shift with little to no sleep." He checked the clock on the wall. He had slept for four hours.

"You know the course at the country club is cleared every morning."

He sat up as his mother continued to talk. He threw the comforter to the side and put his feet on the floor. "It's cold outside, Mother. The club does not have heaters on the course."

"Your father loves the cold weather. He says it's invigorating."

"My father is of the Caucasian persuasion. He likes the cold. I took after your side of the family, I like heat." Theo stood, put his slippers on and walked into his bathroom.

"You have his blood as well as mine."

"I tend to lean towards my African-American heritage more."

"That has nothing to do with your heritage."

He began to urinate. "There are cultural differences as you point out each time we have a conversation about the women I date."

"It's not about the color of their skin. It's about their upbringing. The stock they come from is important. You are a doctor for goodness sake. You need someone who is articulate, intelligent and of course beautiful. Someone deserving." There was silence. "Are you urinating while I'm on the telephone?"

"Yes, Mother. This is what happens when you call someone before they are able to take care of their daily constitutions."

"Theodore Jefferson Prentiss, where are your manners? I know I taught you better than that."

"You did, Mother. However, you have not learned some of your own lessons. Such as not calling a person's home at an ungodly hour."

"You are worse than your father."

"I know, Mother. We do it because it irritates you. Don't you know that by now?" He flushed the toilet, and then washed his hands.

Sounding disgusted, Leonora Prentiss huffed. "Why you or your father want to annoy me is unclear."

"It's because we love you unconditionally and you have an adorable blush when you get upset with us."

"Well, if that's the reason, I guess I can put up with a little teasing." He could hear the smile in her reply. "I spoke with Liza Marks last night. She said Lorraine is in the office today. You should stop by to say hello since you are off."

He looked heavenward and closed his eyes for a moment. "It doesn't matter how sweet you say it, I am not in need of legal assistance, therefore I have no reason to seek Lorraine out." He walked into the kitchen, put a pod into the Keurig, pushed the button then leaned against the counter to wait for his morning cup of tea.

"My birthday celebration is next week. You will need a date. I think Lorraine will be perfect for you."

"I have a date." He flinched as he told the lie.

"That's wonderful, Theodore. Who is she?"

The guilt ate at him as he heard the excitement in her voice. "No one you know, Mother." At least that part was true for he had no idea who she was.

"Will I get to meet her before the party?"

"Not sure about that. The hospital is calling. I will talk with you soon." He disconnected the call before she could ask another question. The thought of lying to his mother cut him a little. Despite her meddling ways, he knew she meant well. He smiled as he prepared his tea with raw sugar, with a touch of lemon juice. His father always said, *You would think after we went through hell to be together, your mother would know better than to interfere in your love life. However, she does not. My suggestion is you take the same position your parents took. Marry for love, for nothing else will get you through the tough times like love.'*

Theo's cell phone rang interrupting his thoughts as he sat at his kitchen table with his tea. This time he checked before answering.

"Morning, Vinnie. Did you get the car?"

"You know I should charge you extra for asking me to put this piece of junk in my showroom. You know I only work on vehicles. I'm not sure what this atrocity is called."

Theo laughed at the man he had known all his life, who, despite his contrary expression could repair anything mechanical placed before him. "Can you make it run again?"

"There is no reason for insults, Theo. Of course I can. I may have to rebuild a part or two. I'm certain the manufacturers no longer carry parts for a 1989 Maxima. This car has over 300,000 miles on it. Who does this beast belong to?"

"A woman I picked up in the hospital garage last night."

"Is she as old as the beast? You know we are in the twenty-first century now. She needs to upgrade."

"No, she is not. How soon can you have it ready?"

"It may take a minute. I'll have to call around to a number of junkyards to see if they have the parts I need. If I find what I need it will only be a temporary fix. The lady may want to consider purchasing a vehicle." Theo heard a bang, then the roaring of a motor. "See that, it likes the Flintstone's style of repairs. One good bang and she's ready to go."

Theo couldn't stop from laughing. Memories of Pearl banging on the car last night didn't help. "How long?"

"Not sure. It's going to take a miracle. Maybe a few days."

"Give me a call when the miracle is ready." Theo hung up the telephone as he thought about Pearl's reaction to the news. He smiled as he dialed the number he put in his cell phone, wondering if her reaction would be as rambunctious as it had been last night. It would give him the opportunity to kiss her again. And he desperately wanted to kiss her again.

"Good morning, Mrs. Lassiter, this is Theo Prentiss from last night. Is Ms. Lassiter awake?"

"Hello, Dr. Prentiss. Pearl and her father left when he came in this morning from work. He plans to take her home then to work this morning. Do you have information on her car?"

"Yes, ma'am. It's going to take a few days to find the parts."

"I was afraid of that. Pearl has been driving that car since Joshua gave it to her in high school. Joe has told her she needs to get a new car."

"That is the advice from my mechanic. He believes he can repair it, however, he is just as certain it will break down on her again. Do you think she will be open to getting a new car?"

"Of course not," Sally laughed. "Pearl hates change of any kind. The only way she will give up that car is if one of her brothers gives her another one."

"Tight on a dollar?"

"No, just plain old stubborn," Sally laughed.

Theo nodded as he agreed with Sally's assessment of her daughter. "Yes, received a taste of that last night."

"So I noticed," Sally replied.

Theo smiled. He was certain she was referring to the kiss in the doorway. "Well, she is as beautiful as she is stubborn."

"That she is."

He could hear the smile in her voice. "I don't mean to cross any boundaries here, but I was wondering if there is a second vehicle she can use until hers is repaired? If not, she can use one of mine."

There was silence on the other end of the telephone. "How kind of you, Dr. Prentiss. I'm certain she will appreciate your thoughtfulness. Here, let me give you her address, her cell phone number and her work number so you can contact her directly."

Theo took down the information as Sally continued to talk.

"Pearl loves her independence. Do you think you will need anything else? Shoe size? Dress size? Ring size?"

Theo laughed. "Anything further I'll get from her, thank you."

"You do that, Dr. Prentiss. While you are at it, think about joining us for dinner on Sunday. We'll be decorating the house for the holidays."

"Thank you for the information and the offer. Would you be offended if I wait for an invitation from her?"

"You may be waiting for a while. Keep in mind the door is always open here."

"I appreciate that, Mrs. Lassiter. I'll talk with you soon."

Theo hung up the phone wondering what decorations they had to do. The tree was up and the stockings were hung. He shrugged the thought away as his mind began to envision the shock on Pearl

Lassiter's face when he showed up at her job with a car. To his surprise, his heart skipped a beat at the anticipation of seeing her again.

Chapter 4

Pearl was finally living the life she wanted. After graduating with a degree in Mass Communications she found herself working at a local radio station. It was fun, however, the pay wasn't great. She had student loans to repay and younger brothers and sisters to help through college. More so, she found herself butting heads with the program director because of her political views. She needed more. Pearl went back to school to receive a Master's in Public Policy and Administration. Two weeks after graduation she walked into the office of James Brooks and was hired as the Press Secretary for JD Harrison's campaign. Her life had meaning and she was determined not to allow anything or anyone to interfere with her career plans. She had disappointed her parents once in life and she vowed to never do it again.

"Daddy, thank you for taking me to the office. I'm so sorry for this. I know you are tired."

"Pearl, I'm your father. I would do anything for you."

She turned in her seat and looked out the window of her father's truck. "I'll check on my car first thing."

"It's not an issue, Pearlie. I can come by and pick you up this evening."

"No, Daddy, you need your sleep. I'll work something out if my car isn't ready."

"Have you spoken with Dr. Prentiss this morning?"

"Not yet. He should have called to tell me where my car is by now. Leave it to a man to be so inconsiderate."

Joe smiled inward not daring to offend his daughter. She sure was hard on men. Ever since that boy from high school left her, no one had stood a chance...until now. The look on his daughter's face when the doctor kissed her was priceless. He had played it over and over in his mind since it happened and he knew Dr. Theodore Prentiss would be his son-in-law one day, if he could get through the foolishness and see the beautiful gem.

"Hmm." He would have to get Joshua to check the man out.

"Did you say something, Daddy?"

"You should give him a call. If I remember correctly he had just gotten off a long shift when he stopped to help you. He may still be sleeping."

"That's no excuse to be inconsiderate. He should have known I needed my car to get to work this morning."

"How would he know that, Pearl? Did you tell him?"

"No."

She thought about it for a moment. Giving her father a little hope.

"People have to work for a living. They need transportation to get to work. The good doctor should have been able to decipher that on his own."

Joe laughed. "You sure are hard on a man who stopped to help you in the middle of the night, brought you home then gave you a kiss good night." He pulled over in front of her office building. "I want you to think about something. You are a stranger to him. He came to your rescue. Give this man the benefit of the doubt. In fact, to thank him for his kindness you should invite him to Sunday dinner."

Pearl turned to her father, appalled. "I will not invite him anywhere. The man is an uppity suburbanite. All I want from him is my car."

"I think you want a little more. Now, give your father a kiss and have a good day at work."

Pearl bent over and kissed her dad on the cheek. "I don't want anything from the good doctor."

"I think you protest a bit too much," he said as Pearl stepped out of the truck. "I'll tell your mother to expect the doctor for Sunday dinner."

"Daddy," Pearl huffed as he pulled away from the curb and drove off.

As she turned to walk into the building, she noted the sidewalk had been cleared of snow and ice from the night's snowfall. For this, she was grateful. The red four-inch pumps she wore today were for cuteness, not weather. She kept telling herself she did not dress for Theo this morning. However, she did put on her navy sheath dress that accentuated the contours of her body to a point of distraction for men. She released the twist she put in the night before allowing the natural curl of her hair to hang around her neck, with a hairband holding it back from her face, giving the high cheekbones, dark brown eyes and double dimples the opportunity to shine without hindrance. The look wasn't new to Pearl. She had her own style of chic and professional. This dress, however, was to attract attention. Her point was proven as she removed her coat, after walking into the front doors of the Harrison Campaign office. Every conversation in the room ceased as she walked towards her office.

"Good morning, Christine." Pearl smiled as she stopped at the front desk to speak with her secretary.

She picked up the messages and began to sort through them.

"A few calls from reporters on the accident involving Cynthia Thornton. Mr. Brooks called indicating he will be in around nine. He left a few suggestions for a press conference to respond to any questions on the accident. Also, Mr. Thompson called. He's stopping by the hospital this morning, but will be in for the staff meeting." She paused for a moment. Then handed Pearl another message. "A Dr. Prentiss called." She held the message between them. "He wants to know if you are free for lunch?" Christine raised an eyebrow as she asked the question. "That dress is saying you are. So...who's Dr. Prentiss?"

Pearl pulled the message from the woman's hand. "Thank you. Please call the AG's office. Ask Calvin Johnson if he can make the staff meeting. We'll keep it short."

"Will do? Who is Dr. Prentiss?"

Pearl began to walk away as she replied. "My biz." She smirked, then continued to her office.

"The dress is working," Christine stated to her back.

Pearl hung her coat up, then dropped all the messages but the one from Dr. Prentiss on the desk. Staring at the number she debated on calling him back now, or waiting. The truth was her body was still calling out from that kiss. She would be lying to herself if she said it did not affect her. If anyone asked could you get an orgasm from a kiss the answer is HELL YES. For that reason her mind was telling her to get her car and stay as far away from that man as she could. He had the power to cause damage and her heart had been broken once before. She wasn't going to let it happen again. Her mind cried out, BUT THAT KISS.

She put the message with the others on her desk and pulled up her computer to check news reports and online blogs to see what was being broadcast on the Attorney General today. She also had to work on his holiday speeches and appearances. The weeks between Thanksgiving and Christmas were fun, but busy for a politician. Most were holiday luncheons or dinners so the topics were light. Her job was putting together the right speech for the right audience to bring maximum attention to the AG's agenda. Pearl stopped, turned her music on, then began working. An hour later the meeting alert popped up on her computer screen. She picked up her tablet, and the most recent schedule of appearances for the AG and made her way to the conference room.

The staff meeting ran longer than the normal hour. It was close to eleven when Pearl walked into her office to find Dr. Theodore Prentiss in all his fineness standing at her office window looking out. She saw the arrogant stance and knew it had to be him with his legs braced apart, his hands in his pockets and the cashmere coat hanging loose. It so reminded her of her brother Joshua. Then he turned around. Pearl almost lost her balance. It was a good thing Brian was walking in behind her, for if he hadn't been she would have fallen flat on her face. To say the man was fine would not give him any justice whatsoever. Why didn't she notice last night the magnificent golden brown skin, with the light hazel eyes and the thick delectable lips. Yes, those were the weapons he'd used against her last night.

"Good morning, Ms. Lassiter."

Did he sound that sexy last night? She hesitated at the door. "Good morning." She gathered herself. "I take it my car is ready?"

Pearl walked over to her desk. That's when Theo got the full impact of her - the beautiful dark mahogany skin that he knew from experience was smooth to the touch, the dark brown eyes that seemed to touch his soul when directed on him. And those lips, that were covered in ruby red lipstick that did not seem flamboyant on her. They looked delightfully stunning. But it was the dress that was ravishing from the front and damn right sinful from behind. He had to take a step back to gather his emotions. That's when he noticed the man standing behind her admiring the same view he was.

Theo extended his hand. "Theodore Prentiss, and you are?"

Brian reluctantly shook the man's hand. "Brian Thompson."

Theo looked from Brian to her. "Am I interrupting something here?"

Pearl looked from him to Brian, then realized she was in the middle of a standoff. "No. We just finished a staff meeting."

"Is the meeting continuing in your office?"

"There are a few things we need to discuss." Brian took a menacing step towards Theo.

"Is it something that can wait?" He turned slowly from Brian to Pearl.

"Do you have some information on my car?"

"Oh, you're the mechanic?" Brian smirked.

"No, I'm not."

"Then who in the hell are you?"

"Someone who came to see me, not you." Pearl stood. "We'll meet later in your office, where you are leaving to go to.... now."

Brian hesitated, then slowly turned to walk out. "I'll be upstairs if you need me."

"She's good," Theo stated as he closed the door then turned to Pearl. "Is there a reason you did not return my call?"

Pearl sat behind her desk, and motioned for Theo to do the same. "I've been in a staff meeting all morning. I planned to return your call once that was complete. However, you beat me to it."

"I'm impatient." He took a seat in front of her desk.

"So I see. Do you have information on my car?"

"I do." He nodded and unbuttoned his suit jacket. "You need a new one."

Pearl sat back with a huff, but could not help admiring the spread of his chest through his white collared shirt. She was tempted to peel the outer coat and suit jacket from his shoulders to see just how broad they were. "I really don't want to buy another car."

"I gathered as much. However, according to my mechanic, even if he makes the repairs the car will malfunction, again. He is searching for the replacement part, which may take him a few days."

"Days?" She stood in a huff. "I need my car. I don't want to depend on anyone else to get me back and forth to work. Do you know how many stops I have to make throughout the day? I can't wait days for my car."

The woman had a healthy set of lungs. He wondered if she was a singer who had to project. He remained calm. "Your mother mentioned that would be an issue for you."

"You're damn right it's an issue."

There was a knock on the door. "Ms. Lassiter, the Attorney General is on line two for you."

Pearl's stomach lurched. "Damn." She took a seat, calmed herself then took a deep breath. "Excuse me for a moment."

The transformation was unbelievable. One moment she was a raving lunatic over the car and now she sat before him, poised and perfectly calm.

Pearl cleared her throat then picked up the receiver. "Good morning, sir."

Theo watched as she nodded her head as she listened.

"I understand your concern. However, I want to reiterate cooler heads prevail here. Any response from you other than what I provided will cause the situation to go negative quickly. That in turn will give the organization more airtime. That is not our goal. Here, we are going to allow the public to be outraged on your behalf. When you speak it should be on the freedom of speech that extends to everyone, even those who oppose you."

She paused and listened. A smile appeared as she nodded in agreement to what was being said on the other end of the telephone. "This is why you pay me the big bucks, to keep you from exploding." She listened again, then replied, "Anytime, sir." She disconnected the call then sat back. She thought for a moment, then picked up the telephone. "Christine, get me everything you can find on The Alliance for America. I want to know where its funding is coming from."

This time she hung up the telephone and turned to him. "This isn't going to be a pretty day."

"What do you do for the Attorney General?"

"I'm his press secretary."

"Ahh yes, you talk to people." He smiled. "For JD Harrison, Attorney General of Virginia?"

"Who will be Governor in a few years and President of The United States of America. Yes, I do. Speaking of which, may I speak with your mechanic about my car?"

Theo hesitated, then stood and took her coat from the hook. "I thought you would make that request."

"We can't simply call him?"

"You appear to be the type that only believes when seen with your eyes."

Pearl stood to allow him to help her with her coat. "You, Dr. Prentiss, know me so well."

"Not yet," he whispered in her ear. "But I will and soon." He raised an eyebrow and opened the door.

The two walked through the office with her co-workers watching. They were a striking couple, her in a long white winter coat and he in a contrasting black. That wasn't what caught their attention. It was the smile that lit up Pearl's face that gave them all a warm feeling.

"Wait here. I'll get the car."

"I can walk with you."

Theo looked down at her feet, then back up to her face. "I have a feeling those shoes are for looks, not walking. I'll be right back." He smiled as he walked out the door.

Pearl found herself watching as he crossed the street to enter the parking deck.

"Dr. Theodore Prentiss. The top trauma surgeon at the Medical College Hospital and the youngest in his field." Brian stood behind Pearl. She turned to stare at him. "You don't go after Scrubs, do you?"

"I don't go after anyone," Pearl said as she turned to face him. "I didn't go after you."

"See, we were friends with a mutual need. No strings, just good sex."

"Excuse you, I gave you great sex." She grinned then turned back to watch for Theo.

"You did." Brian touched her on the shoulder. When she turned he was serious. "He seems like a good brother on paper. If he turns out to be a decent human being, give him a chance for something more than great sex. You deserve more." He kissed her cheek. "Hmm, Mercedes C-Class." He shrugged. "He could do better than that." Brian grinned and walked away just as Theo parked.

Theo opened the car door as she stepped outside. "How many vehicles do you have?" Pearl asked before getting in.

"A few." Theo smiled.

"Some people are struggling to keep one."

Theo stepped closer to her and held her eyes with his. "Yes, there are. I am not one of them. I went to medical school. Learned a lot, obtained a skill that allows me to save lives. It's been hard, grueling at times. However, I persevered and am now a physician, which can be lucrative. I will not apologize or explain for what I have obtained in life. For I know the opportunity to do the same exists for every person in this United States. Now, I want you to think that through before you start your soapbox on the haves and the have nots." He raised an eyebrow. "Shall we go?"

Pearl held his glare for a long moment. She then pulled her coat together and sat in the silver C-class Mercedes sedan.

They met with the mechanic, whose lobby looked more like a showroom, than a body shop. She liked the mechanic immediately, he was funny and straight to the point.

"Your car is a piece of junk that has seen better days. It's given you well over 300,000 miles. It's time to put it out of its misery."

"I need a new car," Pearl conceded.

"Yes, my queen, you do." Vinny smiled. "I can fix it, but it will be a waste of your money. You'll have to come see me again in about three months. Now, as much as I like the idea, it would be unethical."

Pearl exhaled. "Alright. What do I owe you for your services?"

"Oh, I don't know. How about a good meal for my drooling friend over here."

"I don't drool," Theo protested. "And I don't need you begging for food for me. I can beg myself."

"I don't know." Vinny shook his head. "If I had a woman in my car that looked like that, I wouldn't be at no mechanic's shop. No, sir. I'd be at the best steak house in town with candlelight and you." He pointed to Pearl.

"Where have you been all my life, Vinny? I'm a girl who loves a good steak."

"Is that so?" Theo smiled. "I would have taken you for a vegetarian."

Pearl put her hand on her hip. "It takes a lot more than veggies to keep these curves in place."

"Amen and pass the biscuits, please." Vinny laughed.

"In that case, Ms. Lassiter, will you join me for lunch at the finest steak establishment in Richmond?"

There was something special about Theodore Prentiss. He'd captured her curiosity with that smoldering stare and that entrancing smile. "You think you can handle lunch with me, Dr. Prentiss?"

He strolled towards her, with a sense of ownership radiating from him. He gently kissed her lips. "Why don't you get your things out of your car and put them in mine. Then let's go to lunch and find out who can handle who."

It took every ounce of restraint she had not react to the simple kiss. But damn if he did not have some soft lips. "I'll comply because I'm hungry." She turned towards the car. "But don't be walking around thinking you can just kiss me anytime you feel like it."

Theo stood there watching as she pulled items from the trunk and glove compartment of her car as Vinny walked up behind him.

"I hope you're ready. She's a keeper." He patted Theo on the back. "Please invite me to dinner when you introduce her to Leonora. I don't want to be a fly on the wall for that one. I want a front row seat." Vinny laughed as he walked off.

"Front row seat to what?" Pearl asked as she approached with a box in her hands.

Chapter 5

It was now after noon and the restaurant was crowded. It was the type of establishment one did not walk into without a reservation and expect a table. However, as Pearl soon discovered, Theo Prentiss was not an ordinary man.

"Good afternoon, Dr. Prentiss. Would you like your regular table?" the Maître'd asked as he removed the red rope divider.

"Good afternoon, Mr. Quartz. Is the Sky Room available?"

The Maître'd checked the seating chart. "Yes, it is." He pushed a button, then turned to them with a smile. "Right this way."

Pearl looked behind her to see several people waiting. She whispered, "Theo, there are people waiting to be seated that were here when we arrived."

He took her hand and kept walking. "That's true."

They took the elevator up two floors and were escorted to a private dining room. The view of the city appeared before them. In the center of the room was a table set for two. Smooth R&B was playing in the background. Beautiful red poinsettias were strategically placed throughout the room with a magnificent Christmas tree dressed in silver bells and red bows. The fragrance was wonderful.

"May I take your coats?" A waiter appeared from out of nowhere.

"Yes, of course." Pearl took off her coat and handed it to the man as did Theo. "Thank you."

"My pleasure." He disappeared just as quickly as he had appeared with both coats.

Theo held out a chair for her. She smiled, then took the seat. "I must say, this is a bit much for just lunch."

Theo took the seat across from her. "I have a feeling nothing is too much for you, Ms. Lassiter."

The waiter recited the menu to them. After they placed their order, Theo shook out the linen napkin and placed it across his lap. "Tell me about yourself, Ms. Lassiter."

"Why do you insist on calling me Ms. Lassiter?" Pearl popped the napkin open, then placed it on her lap.

"I don't recall you giving me permission to call you by your given name."

"Are you serious? You are waiting for me to say you can call me Pearl?"

"Yes."

"And if I don't?"

"Manners 101. When first introduced to a person they should be addressed as Ms., Miss, Mrs., or Mr. followed by their surname, unless it is a child. To do differently is considered a sign of disrespect."

"You've kissed me twice in less than twenty-four hours. I think we can drop the formalities."

"Be careful, Ms. Lassiter. I think you are beginning to like me. Could trust be next?"

"I stopped trusting boys when I was sixteen years old, Dr. Prentiss."

"Then it's a good thing I'm not a boy."

The waiter appeared with the wine. He poured a small amount in a glass and waited for Theo to give his approval. He nodded. The waiter filled both glasses then walked away.

"Did I offend you a moment ago?"

"No. I simply stated a fact. I am not a boy. I'm a man who recognizes a gem when I see one."

"Really?"

"Yes. I rarely let a treasure slip away and, Pearl Lassiter, you are indeed a treasure to behold."

"You can tell that in the short day you've known of my existence?" she asked sarcastically.

"Your smart words are a facade, a barrier you put up to hide what's inside."

"I'm not that transparent, Doctor Prentiss."

"To the average man you are not." He sat forward. "You will soon learn there is nothing average about me."

Pearl met him halfway across the table as she leaned in. "Let's be clear. I am as attracted to you as you are to me. We will have sex." She put up a finger. "Great sex, but don't expect to get inside my head, Dr. Prentiss. When I've had my fill, we will say our thank yous and go our separate ways."

Theo sat back and stared at her for a long moment.

"Did I render you speechless?" Pearl boasted with a chuckle.

"No. You gave me the reason for your shield. I'm thinking through my next move."

"Since you are so insightful, please share my reasons."

"Thank you. Here's what I see. Somewhere in your past you were hurt. I'm thinking by the boy you lost trust in when you were sixteen. That's the reason for your harsh judgment on all mankind."

The waiter placed their food on the table. "Will there be anything else, Dr. Prentiss?"

"No, thank you."

"I'm not judgmental."

Theo laughed at that. "You are cruelly judgmental when it comes to me. Within hours of knowing me you called me a snob, an elitist and a liar."

"You are an elitist. Look at what took place when we arrived here. There are at least ten people waiting to be seated and yet, they took you within a minute of our arrival. And you expected to be placed before others. That's being an elitist."

"When I own the place I do expect to be treated a little differently by my staff. The reason there are always people waiting to be seated is because of the way my staff treats every person who walks in the door. Patrons return because they know their wait will be less than ten minutes of their arrival or their meal is free. It's called good business. You called it being an elitist because you are judgmental."

"How was I supposed to know you owned the place?"

"Try asking. Take a moment to get to know who I am before whirling accusations around." He cut into his steak and took a bite, then put his fork down. "I've helped you when you were stranded, took you home, came to your place of employment to take you to your vehicle and now I've taken you to lunch. Not once have you said thank you. You call me an elitist, but you are the one acting like you are entitled." He stood and dropped his napkin on the table. "Enjoy your meal," he said as he walked away.

Pearl watched as he spoke with the waiter. She had to have told him thank you at some point, didn't she? Had she been that rude to him? Her parents would be so disappointed in the way she had treated someone who had done nothing but help her from the moment they met. She should go to him and apologize. But wouldn't that show weakness? She saw the waiter hand Theo his coat.

"Theo, wait." She walked over and exhaled. The waiter disappeared. Pearl looked up into expectant eyes. Beautiful, blazing eyes with a tad bit of impatience. "Thank you for your help with my car. I have a tendency to forget my manners at times. It's not an excuse, but a fact. Please forgive me. I would really like to finish our lunch, together."

Theo saw the uncertainty in her eyes. He didn't like seeing it there. She was such a feisty woman and he liked her that way.

"I did more than help you with your car. If I remember correctly, I gave you one hell of a kiss, twice." Pearl gave him that full dimpled smile and his world melted.

She stepped to him and whispered against his lips, "Dr. Prentiss, believe me, any kiss I give, you will remember." She kissed the corner of his lips, put her arms around his neck, then proceeded to prove her statement.

The coat fell to the floor as his arm circled her waist, their bodies merged and their tongues explored the sweet taste of a new love on the horizon.

Theo broke the kiss, but held her to him. "I love a challenge, Pearl. I don't scare easily."

Pearl touched his lips with her finger, then slowly walked back to the table. "Good, because I love a good chase."

He could not help but to notice the movement of her body in that dress. But it was the legs that seemed to go on forever that did him in. "How great is the sex?" he asked as he retook his seat to finish lunch.

They talked for hours about her family, his family, college days, their careers and their future expectations. By the time they left the restaurant it was close to three.

"I enjoyed lunch, but I really need to get back to the office," Pearl explained as she buttoned her coat.

Theo opened the car door for her. "My place is five minutes away. You can drop me off on the way."

"Drop you off?" Pearl questioned.

Theo walked around and climbed into the driver seat. "Yes. Your things are already in here. You can drive this until you get a new car."

"Theo," a shocked Pearl exclaimed. "I can't drive your car."

"Of course you can, it's an automatic."

"It's also a Mercedes. I can't afford to pay for it if something happens."

"Are you planning on crashing it?"

"No, but..."

"There are no buts." He pulled away from the curb. "You need transportation to do all those important things you do for Harrison. I have several vehicles. Loaning you this one will not hamper me in any way."

"That's not the point. You don't know me. I might be a drug dealer and use your vehicle for a drop or something."

Theo laughed. "You said your brother is an ex-Navy Seal, your other brother works for the CIA, you work for Harrison. I don't think you are into anything illegal. Besides, I met your parents. I know you better than you think."

"Theo, I can't take your car."

"Good because I'm not giving it to you," he said as he pulled into a residential complex with a parking garage. He parked next to his SUV and stopped. "I'm loaning it to you. Tomorrow is Saturday. Do you have any appearances with Harrison?"

"Attorney General Harrison, and no, I don't."

"Good we'll go looking for a car tomorrow."

"You don't have to do that. My father and/or brothers can take me."

He turned to face her in the car. "Pearl, I want to spend time with you. Looking for a car is just a ruse."

"Are you good at making deals?"

"Terrible. I just buy what I like. However, for you I will relinquish my elitist attitude and bargain for you." He kissed her gently on the lips. "I like doing that."

"Do you?"

"I do," he said then got out of the vehicle. "Now, bring your fine self around here and make my driver's seat look good."

Pearl hesitated as she stepped out of the vehicle.

"It's only for a few days. Unless you really don't ever want to see me again, in which case, I can understand you turning my offer down." He hit her with that enticing smile again.

"You are just too damn good looking for your own good," she huffed as she circled the vehicle. She took off her coat and placed it in the backseat, before getting in.

He closed the door as she looked around, then rolled down the window. "You have my number. Call me later and we'll make plans for tomorrow."

"What are you doing this evening?" she asked.

Theo smiled. "Ahh, I have your interest. That's good. I'm going to bed. I'm working off four hours of sleep in the last three days." He bent down. "We'll talk in the morning." He kissed her then hit the top of the car. "Go to work."

Pearl adjusted the seat, then pulled off. Theo started to walk away when she stopped and called out, "Do you have any plans for Sunday?"

"No." He smiled.

"Would you like to join my family for dinner? It will probably only be my parents, little sister and a few brothers."

"I would love to."

"Okay." She smiled. "Get some rest. We'll talk more about it tomorrow. Now, let's see if I can get some wheelies in this ride."

Theo smiled as she pulled out of the garage. He liked her...a lot.

Chapter 6

"Why in the hell is everybody home?"

"You are bringing a man home for Sunday dinner." Ruby laughed. "Everybody wants to witness this miracle."

"It's not a miracle, it's just dinner."

"You're driving the man's Mercedes for goodness sake." Jade smirked. "I'd say that's more than just dinner."

Diamond, her roommate and middle sister, hugged her. "We just want to give you some support."

"According to Phire, you may need a little help with this one." Opal smiled with a raised eyebrow.

"All I said was, he was hot and knew how to tongue you down." She snapped her fingers as her sisters laughed.

"You had no right to tell them anything." Pearl scowled at her youngest sister. "That was my business."

"You made it my business when you decided to make out in the hallway instead of getting a hotel room somewhere."

"Phire." Pearl raised her hand to snatch her little sister, when Ruby, the oldest interceded.

"No, no, no. You can't do that when she is right." Ruby sat Pearl down. "Now listen. It's time for you to spill it." She sat on the bed while the other sisters gathered around.

"Yes, I want dirt." Jade nodded.

"Phire said he's a yum-yum with money." Opal asked, "Is that true?"

"We don't really care about things like that," Diamond stated. "Is he a nice person?"

"The heck with that," Phire laughed. "I want to know if he can lick it up, and rub it down?" All her sisters turned to her with frowns. "Well, he looks like he can," Phire responded to their stares.

"Pearl," her mother's voice penetrated the stairs. "Dr. Prentiss is here."

All of Pearl's sisters jumped up to run to the door. Ruby stopped everyone.

"Mommy said Pearl. Everyone else move back."

Pearl walked over to the door. "Thank you," she said to Ruby. "What is wrong with y'all?" She frowned at her sisters.

"We can't believe you have a man and we don't," Jade stated.

"What?" Pearl questioned.

"Pearl, you treat men like dirt," Opal added.

"It's not that." Diamond moved between her younger sisters and Pearl. "It's just we're all curious about Dr. Prentiss." She turned Pearl by the shoulder. "Let's go downstairs so we can start decorating the outside." Diamond gave her other sisters a warning look. They made a face back at her as they followed Pearl downstairs.

Theo stood in the family room with five giants and Joe. At six-two, Theo never felt intimidated. Today was different. The men were menacing and that, Theo thought, was being nice.

"You're here to see Pearl?" Adam questioned with a curious look. "Why?"

"I happen to like her."

"Pearl?" Mathew asked.

"Yes, Pearl," Theo replied, standing with his coat on and gloves in his hands.

"Pearl?" Timothy asked. "Not Ruby or Diamond?"

"I don't know Ruby or Diamond."

"And Pearl invited you here?" Joshua asked as he circled Theo looking him up and down. "You like torture?"

"Not one of my favorite things," Theo replied following Joshua's motions.

"Then why in the hell are you interested in Pearl?" Joshua stopped in front of him. "If you have spent any time with her you already know her opinion of men."

"She has shared that with me several times."

"Yet, you are here."

Theo looked the threatening man in the eyes. "I am and plan to be around for a while."

"If it's okay with me," Joshua added to Theo's statement.

"No, if it's okay with Pearl. I'm not trying to get with you or your brothers. I'm trying to get with her."

"Oh, you're a cocky one," Mathew stated.

"No." Theo held Joshua's glare. "I know what I want. I tend not to allow obstacles to get in my way."

Samuel and Joe shared a glance and a nod. "Dr. Prentiss, let me have your coat." Samuel walked past his brothers to take the extended coat. "Pearl should be down in a minute. I'm certain she will have a few words for her brothers." Each of them, with the exception of Joshua, grumbled then stepped away.

"I've checked you out." Joshua held his position. "Why haven't you married Lauren?"

When in the hell did he have time to check him out? Theo thought. *He just agreed to dinner on yesterday. And where in the hell did he learn about Lauren?*

"I don't get a rise from Lauren."

"Whoa." Mathew stood. "Don't talk about my sister like that."

"News flash. Your sister is fine."

Mathew grinned as he sat back down. "Damn right, she is."

"Is that what this is, you trying to get with her sexually?" Joshua asked.

"If that was the case I would have done that days ago and wouldn't be here dealing with the third degree."

"We are round one and the light weights," Joshua huffed. "We are just getting you warmed up."

Theo looked around the room. "It feels a bit toasty in here already."

"It's about to get hotter, Dr. Prentiss," Joe stated as he heard the girls coming down the stairs. "Brace yourself."

"You made it." Pearl smiled when she walked into the room. As much as she loved her brothers, Theo captured her complete attention. His smile seemed to brighten his features but then she noticed his eyes were dark, almost ominous. She looked around at her brothers, who were all seated on their sofa. "What did you do?"

"Intimidate him. Exactly what we are supposed to do," Joshua replied.

"You know the routine, Pearl," Joe stated as he sat on the sofa at the top of the semi-circle of sofas. "Come and sit beside me and let the gems and gents do what they do."

Ruby pulled a chair from the dining room and sat it in front of the fireplace as the girls sat on the remaining sofa. "Have a seat, Dr. Prentiss."

There was something in the tone of her voice that caused Theo to breathe a little uneasily. Theo, dressed in grey slacks, a burgundy sweater and a grey collar shirt underneath, sat with a curious look at Pearl.

"It's a family thing." Pearl nodded her head reassuringly. "I promise not to let them kill you."

"Hold on, hold on." Sally came running from the kitchen. "I've waited for this session for a long time." She sat next to her husband and clapped her hands. "Pearl, I pray you are ready."

"Yeah, it's payback time." Jade nodded as she crossed her legs.

"Ruby, let's get started. The rolls are in the oven and I don't want them to burn."

Ruby pulled out her notebook and pen, as she stood next to Theo. "We are the Lassiters. If you are going to be involved with one of us you need to know who we are and what we stand for. We in turn need to know about you."

"We have to do this because of Pearl," Phire explained.

"Phire, this benefits all of us," Ruby stated. "Now wait your turn."

Theo crossed his legs in anticipation.

"Dr. Prentiss, excuse the interruption. On the sofa to your right are Samuel, Joshua, Mathew, Timothy and Adam. Luke, who falls between Matt and Timmy, is not present. On the sofa to your left are Diamond, Jade, Opal, and Sapphire. My name is Ruby."

"Men from the bible and gemstones...unique."

"Thank you." Sally smiled at Theo. "I like you already."

Theo returned the smile until he looked up at Ruby. "No butt kissing with the queen."

Theo stopped smiling but wanted to laugh. He only nodded.

"On the head sofa are Joe and Sally, the patriarch and matriarch of this clan. We're going to ask you a series of questions to see if we like you and if you are a good fit." She stared at him. "Each family member gets one question; however, any member can add on any question."

"Do you do this to everyone who wants to date one of you?"

"Yes," they all replied in unison.

"You don't have to do this, Theo." Pearl stood.

Joe pulled her back down. "Yes, he does."

"Have a seat, Pearl." Sally patted her daughter's hand. "You have done this to all your sisters. Now, it's your turn. Go ahead, Ruby."

Pearl shrugged her shoulders at Theo and mouthed, *Sorry.*

"Anything for you, Ms. Lassiter." Theo smiled then looked at Ruby. "Proceed."

"Thank you. Phire, you go first."

"Okay. Simple, Doc. Bid Whist or Spades?"

The question caught Theo off guard. "Whist, of course."

Ruby made a note of his response. "Diamond."

"Romantic comedy, or Thriller?"

Theo thought for a moment. "Thriller."

"Opal," Ruby guided.

"Checkers or Chess?"

"Chess."

"Jade."

"Sexy or Sensual?"

"Sexy."

"CPA or Tax consultant?" Ruby asked.

"CPA."

"Research or Practical?" Adam asked.

"Both."

"You can't do both," Phire stated.

"In this case you can," Adam replied. "To be a good doctor you have to respect the research."

"Are you pre-med?" Theo asked.

Adam nodded. "I'm thinking of going in that direction."

"Good man." Theo reached over and gave Adam a pound.

Ruby walked between them. "No influencing the judges."

Theo threw up his hands. "Sorry, please continue." He winked at Pearl.

"Football or Soccer?" Mathew asked.

"Football."

"Basketball or Baseball?" Timothy asked.

"Baseball." The men groaned.

"I can shoot, but I prefer baseball."

Joshua sat forward. "Guns or Bombs."

"Neither, but if I had to choose, bombs. Why waste time? Take everybody out."

Joshua stood, shook Theo's hand. "He's in."

"He said he preferred neither," Pearl explained.

"But he understands the concept," Joshua pointed out.

"We're not finished." Ruby pushed Joshua to his seat. "Samuel."

Sammy smiled, held his head down in thought. Then looked up. "Marriage or Sex?"

"Marriage. It enhances the sex."

"Can you elaborate, Dr. Prentiss?" Sally asked.

"Of course." Theo sat forward as if giving a lecture. "Sex is a moment of euphoria acquired when two individuals reach a peak of mutual arousal. There is no guarantee from partner to partner that moment will occur for both or even one. In a marriage you have a primary factor which enhances the sexual experience. That factor is love. The thing we all must remember about love is that it is, and always will be the number one factor in life. Think about it. It was God's love that created heaven and earth. It was Sarah's love for her son, which caused the divide between Isaac and his brother Ishmael. Love is such a deep emotion, that it can literally hurt your body, your mind, and your very soul. However, it is also powerful enough to heal. In marriage, imagine your body being controlled by such a powerful source during the act of sex." He nodded his head. "Now, multiply that by 365 days a year or better yet...a lifetime. Do you have any idea how explosive that can be?" He sat back. "Yeah, I'll take marriage over sex as soon as I find the right woman." He stared at Pearl.

The room fell silent. No one moved or said a word...until Phire spoke up. "Okay, did anybody else get all yucky inside?"

Jade and Opal raised their hands as did Adam and Timothy.

"I think I just came," Ruby mumbled.

Theo stood and whispered in her ear, "It was good for me too." He extended his arm. "Shall we have dinner?"

Ruby threw the book behind her, took the arm he offered and walked towards the dining room. Everyone began talking at once as they filed out of the room. Samuel stopped by Pearl and kissed her temple. "He's a keeper." He smiled at her.

Joshua walked by. "Don't mess this up."

"I like him, Pearl." Diamond smiled as she hugged her sister. "I really like him."

Once everyone was out of the room, Pearl looked up at her father. "Daddy, do you like him? I mean really like him?"

"Pearl, do you like him?"

"I don't want to disappoint you again."

He held his daughter back as the others filed into the dining room. "You have never disappointed me. I never condemned you for following your feelings and I never will. What happened in high school was a mistake, a part of learning and growing. It was not something for you to be ashamed of. Stop beating yourself up, Pearl."

"I know, Daddy, but do you like him?"

Joe could see his daughter needed his reassurance. "Yes, I do. But not more than I love you and want you to be happy."

Pearl smiled. "Okay, I'm not making any promises on how this is going to go. We'll see if he knows how to act. You know how men can be."

Joe shook his head as Pearl walked off and Sally joined him. "So, what do you think?"

Joe shrugged. "He's made it this far. Let's see if he makes it through the night."

Dinner at the Lassiter's was beyond descriptive. The food was delicious, but the company was outrageous. It certainly wasn't like dinner at his parents' house. The siblings at this house spoke loudly, often and quite freely. Theo swore he was going to clone Phire to take to his parents' house to loosen up his mother. As for Joshua, the moment they mentioned outside decorations, he literally disappeared. One minute he was there, the next minute he was gone. Theo was granted the duties of the disappeared Joshua and given the task of stringing the roof, wearing dress loafers no less. All in all the evening went well. Theo could swear the lights were so bright he would probably be able to see them from his balcony. He held out his hand as he helped Pearl to the roof from the attic window.

"You okay?" she asked as she sat beside him.

"Better than okay." He put his arm around her shoulders "I like your family."

"You're still alive so I think they like you, too."

"So...I'm the first man you've brought home to meet them."

Pearl pulled her jacket a little closer. "So far." She grinned.

"I'll take that as a good thing." There was silence between them for a minute. He pointed toward downtown. "That's my building to the right."

"I know. You should show me the inside, sometime."

Theo smiled at her shining eyes. "I'd like to show you the inside of me, tonight."

Pearl kissed his cheek. "I'd like to see that."

"Hey, we are getting ready to plug these in, you two might want to get off the roof," Joe's baritone voice filtered up to them.

"Be right down, Daddy."

Theo stood then helped Pearl up. "I must really like you. I'm in the cold, on a roof, in Italian loafers putting up Christmas lights."

"Santa needs a way to find our house."

"I got a Santa for you."

"Ooh, is he naughty or nice?" Pearl asked as she stepped into the house through the window.

Theo ducked inside then kissed her. "He can't wait to show you." They joined the rest of the family that was outside in the front yard.

"Countdown to the 151 proof eggnog." Phire jumped with a cheer.

Joe caught her by the collar. "Turn on the lights."

Everyone laughed as the lights illuminated the outside of the house.

Joe began singing with a surprisingly rich baritone voice. "Hang all the mistletoe. I'm going to get to know you better...this Christmas."

To Theo's surprise the others all joined in to a lively upbeat version of This Christmas. It was the most fun he'd had in years. He couldn't stop himself from joining in, as neighbors came out of their homes to join in with the singing.

Things went up from there. Someone decided to play poker. Theo, to Joshua's dismay, was surprisingly very good at the game. Joshua, the sore loser, didn't take too kindly to giving up his wallet to Theo, but the man had won it fair and square.

"You made the bet, Joshua," Samuel cautioned his younger brother. "Don't get upset because he outsmarted you. Adam folded, that should have told you something. Stop being a sore loser."

"I'm not a sore loser," Joshua declared.

"You are a terrible loser," Pearl added. "I should have warned Theo not to play poker with you. Give him the wallet back, Theo. It's not that serious."

"Oh hell," Timothy mumbled.

"It's a game, Joshua, and he beat you," Pearl teased.

"Hey, look, um I don't want your wallet. It's all good."

"Oh, now my sister is making decisions for you."

"No. I don't see the virtue in having a disagreement about something this trivial." Theo extended his hand to Joshua. "We good?"

"Joshua, behave." Pearl stood. "Let's go, Theo." Theo stepped back to get his coat.

"You running, Theo," Joshua teased.

"Not running. Just man enough to walk away from a volatile situation."

"Samuel," Pearl pleaded.

Samuel handed Pearl the drink in his hand. "Here, Pearl, have a drink, I'll handle this."

Joshua stepped in front of Theo. "You think you are man enough for my sister? Prove it."

Pearl drank the entire contents of the glass in one gulp. She gave the glass to Mathew. "Joshua, no, this isn't necessary."

"Yes, it is, Pearl," Samuel stated as he handed her another glass of wine. "Drink this. We'll handle the Doc."

Pearl gulped down the second glass of wine. Then gave the empty glass to Mathew, who placed another glass in her hand.

Mathew turned to Ruby, who nodded to keep them going. So he filled the empty glass Pearl gave him and waited.

Pearl downed the third glass. She missed Mathew's hand as she passed it back to him. Opal grabbed the glass before it fell to the floor. She took the glass Mathew now held and put it in Pearl's hand. "You get them, Pearl, don't let them hurt your man."

"He's not my man," Pearl slurred as she took the glass.

"He will be before this night is over," Jade laughed.

"Pearl, drink your wine." Timothy stepped forward. "You know how the Lassiter brothers handle men who mistreat our sisters."

"He didn't mistreat me. He just kissed me."

"Did you like it?" Adam asked as he stood next to his other brothers.

Pearl emptied the glass, then looked around at her sisters. "It was good." She nodded.

"It was real good from what Phire told me," Jade laughed. "The man had her speechless."

"I wasn't speechless, it was the orgasm."

Everyone stopped. Even her brothers, who had all surrounded Theo, turned to look at her. Joshua was the first to recover. He gently, or so he thought, pushed Theo. "You giving my sister orgasms?"

Theo's body bumped into Samuel, who pushed him back towards Joshua, who pushed him to Timothy, who pushed him towards Mathew. When he reached Adam he regained his balance.

"Hey, hey, hey," Theo yelled. "The next person who touches me, I'm taking out your kneecap." The men stopped and stared. "Yes, I kissed her into an orgasm." He walked over to face Joshua. He figured if he was going to die tonight it was going to be quick. "I plan on doing it again as soon as I get her out of here." Theo put up his fist. "Who's going to try and stop me?"

Pearl stumbled into the middle. "You got to go through me to get to him," she shouted. "You put a finger on him, Joshua, I'm kicking your behind."

"You would go against your own brothers for this man?" Samuel asked.

Pearl put her hands on her hips. "Damn right!" She stomped her foot and almost tipped over.

Theo reached out, caught her by the waist, then put her behind him. "You will not."

She jumped back in front of him. "I will. My brothers are professional killers. Stay behind me."

He put her back behind him. "I am the man in this relationship. Now stay back."

She jumped back in his face. "Relationship. Who said we are in a relationship?"

"I did. And you damn well better agree for all I've been through tonight."

"No man tells me what to do unless his name is Joe Lassiter."

"I just did and my name is not Joe, it is Theo. You might as well get used to it. You'll be calling it a lot before this night is over."

The two were so into their argument, neither noticed the brothers had sat down, had drinks in their hands and were watching them, amused.

"How dare you speak to me like that? You don't know me well enough to talk to me that way. I will have every one of my brothers take you out, limb by limb, and spread you around the world so no one will ever find your body."

Samuel and Joshua looked at each other. "You leaving the country tonight?"

"Tomorrow morning," Joshua replied then took a drink.

"I'll store him at my place until morning." Samuel took a drink as Joshua nodded.

"Make sure you have plenty of ice on hand," Adam added. "It will help keep the smell down while the body deteriorates."

"I'm a doctor," Theo yelled. "I know how to torture people in ways your brothers could never imagine."

Pearl huffed. "Did you just threaten my brothers?"

"I did."

Pearl brought her fist up to punch him, but Theo grabbed her wrist. That caused Joshua to rise. Samuel pulled him back down as Theo pulled Pearl to him.

His lips crushed down on hers and relentlessly kissed her until her body went limp. Theo put his arm around her waist, pulling her closer, then began to literally ravish her in front of her brothers and sisters.

"Ten points on technique," Ruby yelled.

"Ten on originality." Opal laughed.

"Twenty on execution." Jade clapped.

"Do you think Pearl is alright," Diamond asked.

Samuel smiled. "Pearl is fine."

"How long are we going to let this go on?" Timothy asked.

"Until Pearl drops to her knees." As soon as the words left Joshua's mouth, Pearl slumped in Theo's arms.

"See, now I'm happy. I'm out," Joshua smiled then literally disappeared.

Theo picked her up and turned to her siblings. "Which of you did this?"

Mathew stood and gave Theo a thump on the shoulder. "Have fun tonight."

Ruby took a good look at Pearl. "Or maybe not." She looked up at Theo. "She is going to be pissed in the morning."

"You know, Theo." Diamond stood. "It's okay for Pearl to stay at your place tonight."

"Yeah, we're going to stay at Diamond's and Pearl's place." Opal smiled. "So, have fun."

"You need any help with getting Pearl to the car?" Adam asked.

"I'm good." Theo adjusted Pearl in his arms, as everyone except Samuel left the room.

"You know we wouldn't leave Pearl in just anyone's hands."

Theo nodded. "I know."

"Take care of her. Pearl is unique. There is only one like her." Samuel grabbed Pearl's coat and walked Theo to the car. "You can wake up now."

Before opening her eyes, Pearl asked, "Is everyone gone?"

Samuel nodded and smiled. "Yes, they have all dispersed in one direction or another."

"I don't like that game you and Joshua just played. But thanks for getting us out of there, Sammy." She opened her eyes and smiled.

He looked at Theo. "You owe me one."

"For keeping your brother from kicking my ass or for trusting me with your sister."

"Joshua doesn't kick ass. He kills you," Samuel said and just walked away.

Theo looked down at Pearl. "Interesting family you have."

"Yes, and scary how well you fit right in."

Theo set her on her feet as he opened the car door. "Is that a good thing or bad?"

"I don't know." She looked past him in thought. "I just don't know," she said as she sat in the car.

Theo closed the door then walked to the driver's seat. Before getting inside he looked at the house with the lights beaming, the candles in the windows and the beautiful red bow on the door. He liked the Lassiters. He liked them and their daughter a lot. He got inside the vehicle. "Allow me to show you how good this really is."

Chapter 7

The first thought that entered Pearl's mind when she walked into Theo's condo was bland. The place was beautiful, but...there was no warmth inside. It seemed like a place to just sleep.

She stepped inside the foyer to high ceilings, wall-to-wall windows, elegant hardwood floors, white walls, and no furniture. "Do you live here or is this where you bring women when you don't want to take them to your real home?"

The rumble of his laughter made her smile. "Sorry, I have this habit of saying the first thing that comes to mind."

"That's a little dangerous for someone in your line of work." Theo hung her coat in the closet and stood back and watched her wander around. His main focus was on her jean-clad legs, the curve of her behind.

"True." Pearl nodded as she took a step into the living room. She did a twirl with her arms spread wide. "Nice open concept. A little empty. Don't like furniture?"

"Haven't found what I want."

She turned to face him. "What are you looking for?"

Theo leaned against one of the pillars that separated the living room from the foyer. He stood there taking in the essence of Pearl Lassiter with her natural hair. "Something with a classic look, vibrant with just a touch of excitement."

Pearl held his gaze then looked away. She turned towards the fireplace. "I would place a long sofa here, with an ottoman, no table. A Persian carpet here, in front of the fireplace to sit on to have a glass of wine, and munch on grapes and cheese while we talk." She then walked towards the row of windows. "I would put a chaise here to read, a table next to it and for Christmas, I would put the tree right here in the center for all to see."

"Let's do it."

"Do what?" She turned towards him.

"Let's get a tree, put it up and decorate it."

Pearl stared at him a bit confused. "I thought you were in a hurry to jump into my panties."

"We can do both." He walked over, took her hand and pulled her towards the door. "Live or fake?" Theo asked as he pulled her coat from the closet.

"Live," Pearl replied still not believing.

"Live, it is." He put his coat on then opened the door.

Pearl didn't move. "You really want to do this?"

Theo took a step to her, ran his tongue over her lips, then kissed her. "Yes, I really do."

He saw the confusion in her eyes, then watched as excitement crept in. "Okay." She smiled. "Let's do this."

When they walked back into the condo, it was well after eleven. They carried the tree in and placed it on the floor. Theo ran back out to the car to bring in all the accessories for the tree. Pearl grabbed two of the bags from him as he placed the others on the floor.

"Which bag is the tree stand in?"

Theo went through the bag and pulled out the stand. He then pulled out the tree bag. "Where do you want the tree to go?"

"Right here so it will be in the center of the window." Pearl pointed.

Theo placed the bag on the floor then set the tree stand in the middle. He slid the tree trunk inside the stand, then turned to Pearl. "Is the tree straight?"

"A little to the right, not too far....okay, right there."

"Alright, hold it in place while I tighten the screws into the trunk."

"I'll hold it, but you are pulling the needles from my hair when this is done."

"Sounds fair to me. Now hold it straight." Theo laid on the floor to tighten the screws until the tree was balanced. "Okay, let it go."

Pearl did as he instructed and the tree fell forward.

"Whoa," Pearl exclaimed as she reached out and grabbed the tree. "I don't think it's ready for me to let go." She laughed.

"Okay, hold it again." Theo loosened the screws, adjusted them to the tree again. "Okay, slowly let it go."

Pearl let it go slowly and to her surprise the tree stayed. "Is it secure?"

Theo stood. "Let's check it." He moved the tree, shook it some. "I think it's ready." He stepped back to where Pearl stood. "What do you say we get this baby decorated?"

"Cool." Pearl went through the bags. "We have to check the lights first to make sure they all work."

The next hour the two worked together decorating the tree with the gold and ivory dressings Pearl had selected. The two stared at the tree once it was finished.

"This is a first." Pearl looked as if she had tears in her eyes.

"The first of many." Theo pulled her close.

Pearl stepped out of his grasp. "Don't say things you don't mean. I don't need that." She began picking up discarded package wrappings and bags.

Theo watched, as she kept busy. He wasn't sure but he thought he had just hit on a nerve.

"You have a problem with relationships?"

She was on her knees putting trash into a bag.

"No, I'm saying I don't need a relationship for us to enjoy having sex together."

Theo bent down in front of her, then took her hands in his. "Look at me, Pearl." Pearl looked up. "I'm not just looking for sex." He inhaled and sat on the floor. "My life has been one accomplishment after another. The one thing I don't have is someone to share those moments and others with. I wasn't looking for you or anyone to fill that role. But then you appeared in the middle of the night, banging the hell out of a car, in a mini skirt with legs that extended forever." Pearl smiled. "I knew in that moment that you were out to change my life as I knew it. For the last three days that's exactly what you have done. And I like it. As crazy as it sounds I like you. The mad woman with the crowbar, dangerous brothers and a smart-ass tongue has captured my attention and a little part of my heart. I don't want just sex from you. I want the essence of you. "

The declaration stunned Pearl. She was used to men wanting her for her body and nothing more. She was okay with that because she didn't want them anywhere near her heart. But this man, with his short cropped hair, hazel eyes and delicious lips wanted more and damn if she didn't want to try. It was just... she didn't know if she could. A relationship with someone had been a foreign thought for her. She expected it for others, but never for herself. Now here was Theo asking her to believe in something she'd closed her mind to years ago.

"I'm not good at the long term thing. I'm much better at friends with benefits. It's what I'm used to."

Theo put his hand under her chin and held her face up so she was looking directly at him. "Get used to it. I want an exclusive...one-on-one relationship with you. And I mean to have it."

"How're you going to make me be in a relationship with you?"

"I'm not going to make you do anything. You want this as much as I do. You're just afraid for some reason." He gently kissed her lips. "You want me, Pearl Lassiter. You might as well admit it."

Pearl smiled at him. "Where in the hell did you come from, Dr. Prentiss, and where did you get those compelling eyes? You should have been a lawyer."

"Well the eyes come from my father and the compelling argument is courtesy of my mother. So, what do you say, Pearl Lassiter. Will you be my girlfriend?"

Pearl laughed. "Your girlfriend." She shrugged. "I haven't been a girlfriend in a long, long time."

"Is that a yes or no?"

"You are too cute for your own good."

He smiled, then kissed one corner of her lips. "Is that a yes," he kissed the other corner of her lips, "or a no?"

She sat there a breath away from his lips. "I'll take yes for a hundred."

Theo smiled then pulled her onto his lap. "I like you, Pearl Lassiter."

"I like you, too, Theodore Prentiss."

"Are you ready to turn it on?"

"Yes." Pearl was beaming with excitement.

"Okay, wait, let's turn all the lights off." Theo ran over, turned the main lights off. "Okay, now."

Pearl put the cord to the lights into the socket and the tree came to life. She stood and walked over to his arms that were open and waiting for her. It felt good standing there in silence, enjoying the moment with him. "I think it's time for you to turn me on."

Theo looked down at her. "Come with me." He took her hand and walked from the great room to a hallway behind the fireplace. The hallway had a doorway leading to a kitchen, bathroom, sunroom and at the end was a set of double doors.

Behind the doors was a sitting room with another fireplace with a large screen television mounted above it, floor to ceiling windows and furnished with a burgundy leather sofa, and cocktail table with books scattered on top.

"This is where you spend your time."

"Guilty." Theo held onto her hand and walked through the arch leading to the bedroom. "More time is spent here."

"Aha, Theo's Throne. How many women and how often?"

Theo pulled her to the bed. She sat and laid back. Theo lay on top of her then pulled her legs around his waist. He settled in, and then used his thumbs to caress her cheeks. "One woman, first time."

"You've never had anyone here?" Pearl asked not believing him.

"You are my very first visitor. Know why?"

There was something in his eyes that held her as she shook her head.

"Because I've never wanted to share this part of my life with anyone. You're the only one I've ever thought of in my bed. I've had others in their beds, hotel beds, but never in my bed. Only you."

"Why me?"

"The hell if I know." He smiled. "But here you are. Now, if I remember correctly..." He cleared his throat. "You mentioned something a few days ago about great sex."

Pearl smiled as she wiggled beneath him. "I recall something like that."

"So was that just talk?"

Pearl flipped him over until she was straddling him. She pulled her sweater over her head revealing a purple front clasp, lace bra. "No, Dr., that is a fact." She then pulled his sweater over his head. Underneath he had on a collared shirt. "Okay, two things. One, you've got to stop wearing so much clothing. It takes too long to get you out of them." Theo's hands circled her waist. The warmth of his touch distracted her momentarily. That was new. Men had touched her body before and that particular sensation had never occurred. It took her a second to recover. "Two, if you experience the greatest sex of your life you have to let your hair grow and then have it braided."

His fingers roamed under the bottom of her bra, brushing against her breast. The light touch startled her. "Agreed."

After a few buttons she realized he had on a t-shirt under the collared shirt. "You've got to be kidding me."

Theo laughed. "Hey, I have to make you work for it."

Pearl pulled both shirts over his head. As he lay back down, the smooth caramel skin covering his broad chest and leading to six-pack abs caused her to gasp. She spread her hands across his chest, then down his abs. "You should never hide this," she said as she licked her lips.

Theo unclipped her bra, then pushed it over her shoulders. "You should never hide these." He sat up, ran his thumb across her moist lips, cupped her cheek, then covered her mouth with his.

Their bodies touched. Hot skin to hot skin and both their worlds, as they knew it changed in that instant. Pearl wrapped her arms around his neck as Theo's arms circled her waist. The heat from their touching spread throughout their bodies. Their tongues merged in an exploration of tasting, enticing and savoring the wonder of this new experience.

Theo flipped her onto her back then placed kisses down her cheek, her neck, between her breasts, taking one dark chocolate nipple between his lips. His wet tongue, with the suckling motion of his mouth caused Pearl's body to arch up. Her hands grasped the back of his head encouraging him to take more into his mouth. Theo turned to the other nipple and caressed it with his thumb. He traveled down to her navel, paying homage to the flat stomach, small waist and honey flavored skin. He unbuttoned her jeans, then zipped them open. Next, he pulled her boots, and jeans to the floor. She lay on his white comforter with her mahogany skin, purple lace boy shorts and he thought she was the most magnificent sight he had ever seen. Never taking his eyes from hers, he unzipped and dropped his pants to the floor. "If you experience the best sex in your life, I want you to tell the next five people we see you are in a relationship with me."

Pearl would have agreed to anything as she gazed upon the man in all his glory. He was long, thick and from the looks of things eager to touch her. Pearl's tongue touched her lips as she continued to stare at the wondrous sight of the man before her. God had certainly blessed him with brains, looks and length. "Do I have to use the word?" she asked as she looked up at him.

"Yes." She reached out to touch him, but he stepped back. "Yes or no?"

"Arrgh," she pouted. "Agreed." She licked her lips.

Theo reached into the nightstand and pulled out a condom. He tore open the package then smoothly covered himself. He then bent down and pulled the purple lace panties down her long, shapely legs and dropped them to the floor. Putting his hands behind her knees, he pulled her to the edge of the bed then stepped between her thighs. "Thank you," she said as he entered her in one long, powerful stroke. The feel of her around him rendered him powerless. He could not move. Did not want to move. He wanted to hold this position with her warmth around him forever and a day.

Pearl's eyes closed and she groaned at the feeling of completeness that filled her. Never had a man's entrance rendered her motionless. She wrapped her legs around his waist, pulling him deeper inside of her. She wanted to feel the heat of him throughout her body. "Theo," she moaned.

He immediately fell into her arms. "Pearl."

They were content to lay there, entwined, embracing the arising of something neither was able to articulate. Their bodies took over and instinctively knew exactly what to do. Theo pulled out, then entered her again, this time more powerful than before. Pearl's nails scraped across his back as he branded her over and over again with each thrust.

Their joining wasn't sweet, it was primitive and Pearl was calling out for him to give her more, and more as he pumped furiously, ravishing every inch of her within his reach and some places that weren't. The heat escalated to a scorching point, but neither could stop, they were in a zone where a mixture of sensuality from their raw sex battled for dominance. It was raw sex that won out when Theo pushed up on his hands leaving nothing but his sex inside of her and her legs wrapped around him. He pumped and pumped and pumped until Pearl screamed and her nails bit into his skin. Theo continued until he could not hold back any longer. He exploded with his head thrown back and his breath caught in his throat. He fell on top of her, turned onto his back and brought her over him.

They both lay there struggling to breathe. Then suddenly they both began laughing as they realized both had won the bet.

Later, after they were sated with another round of lovemaking, with their bodies still entwined, Theo caressed Pearl's thigh. "Tell me about him."

"Who?"

"The guy from high school."

Pearl absent-mindedly trailed her finger across Theo's chest. "You don't really want to know."

"Yes, I do. I need to know. It seems to be the one thing that has defined your life over the last few years." He took her fingers in his hand, brought them to his lips and gently kissed them. "For me to understand you, I have to know what happened."

Pearl hesitated, but for the first time the memory of the time did not sadden her or make her feel guilty.

"His name was Lionel Jackson. I loved me some Lionel. I ate, slept and dreamt Lionel. He was king Lionel to me."

"Okay, okay, I get the idea." Theo smiled.

"Yeah, well, I was stupid. He said he loved me and we would be together forever."

"Hmm."

"Yeah, hmm. Well forever was until he laid eyes on Cynthia Thornton, the green eyed vixen that is now engaged to my brother."

"Samuel?" Pearl nodded. "That's who you were visiting in the hospital the night we met."

"Yep." Pearl leaned up on her elbow, propping her head up so she could see his expression when she told him the rest. "He broke up with me at the prom, because after one dance with Cynthia he declared himself in love with her."

"Ouch, he broke up with you at the prom?"

"In the middle of the dance floor when I approached him with her standing there."

"Ooooh."

"His words were, 'Pearl, you're okay, but I have a chance with Cynthia Thornton. She is more than okay. Hell she's beautiful.'"

"What did Cynthia do?"

"She laughed and walked off with her friends to tell them what happened."

"What did Lionel the wonderful do?"

"Ran after her."

Theo sat up on his elbow, facing her. "What did Pearl do?"

"Stood in the middle of the floor looking like a fool. My brother Mathew was there and took me home." She licked her lips. "A few days later I was having cramps and bleeding so Ruby took me to the emergency room. I found out I was pregnant, but had miscarried. My parents were so hurt when I told them. I could see the disappointment in their eyes. Samuel and Ruby took care of me while my parents worked. No one else knew about it. I was sixteen years old. I have spent every year of my life since that time trying to make them proud of me again. Everything I do is geared towards seeing that pride I used to see in their eyes when they look at me. I've stayed away from any man who I thought would be able to control me like that." She looked up at him. "Until you."

Theo exhaled. He put his hands around her waist and pulled her to him. He kissed the tip of her nose, then stared down into her eyes. "I see nothing but pride in your parents' eyes when they talk about you. I can't speak for them, but I'm pretty sure they forgave you the night you came home healthy to them. I think it's you who needs to forgive yourself." He pulled her under him. "I don't know what I've done to earn it, but I treasure you and the trust you've placed in me. It's more precious than silver and gold."

"What about platinum?"

He rubbed his thumb across her brow. "There is not a metal that can compare to you." He kissed her with a gentleness that surged through every pore in her body.

This kiss was different from the others. This kiss felt euphoric. The feeling you get when you know it's the beginning of true love and it scared her senseless. Pearl closed her eyes. She knew she was lost. Theodore Prentiss had gotten under her skin.

Chapter 8

The Confederate Country Club was filled to capacity to celebrate the birthday of Leonora Prentiss. The elites were in the house dressed in their tuxedos and gowns. This was a birthday celebration, but since it was so close to Christmas it was also the annual gathering to ring in the holidays. The who's who of the socialites were in attendance.

Theo could see his mother's spirits were high and she loved the attention. He wondered if he should wait to introduce her to Pearl. It was at that moment his father walked up behind him.

"Too late to change your mind now. Your mother is expecting her and you've already invited her." Edward Prentiss, III clapped his son on the shoulder.

Theo's height, hazel eyes and temperament all came from his father. Edward was one of the most easy-going people a person would ever come across. His patients loved his bedside manner. The hospital applauded his diplomacy and society loved his openness. No one in his immediate circle was surprised when he married a real live Pam Grier figure, Leonora Greene. The two fell in love on the University of Virginia's campus during a time when stares were their greeting at just about every establishment they entered. But neither cared. His parents' union was based on love. That's the one thing he wanted in his life, a love like theirs. He believed that wish was in the making.

"I'm not nervous," Pearl kept repeating to herself as she pulled up to the magnificent white building with pillars in the front, lights all around and the history of Virginia inside. Also known as The

Confederate Country Club. It was not her first time in the establishment, however it was her first time meeting the parents of someone she was involved with. If Theo was just another man this event would not faze her. After last night, she knew he was not just another man; he was the man who made her toes curl, her stomach flop and her vee-jay-jay cream with joy. If there was ever a time she needed the Lord's intervention to keep her opinions to herself if was now. *Please, Lord, hold my tongue. If not for me, do it for Theo. He so wants this meeting to go well.*

Why did she agree to do this? Pearl thought as she waited for the valet to come to the car. *Because Theo caught her in a weak moment when he asked her to attend his mother's birthday party. And for the last week she had not been able to deny him much of anything.*

She stepped out of the car. "Man up. You're a Lassiter, dammit."

Pearl entered the lobby of the country club and was met by two hostesses. One took her coat, the other searched for her name on the attendance roster.

"I'm probably a write-in," Pearl suggested.

The woman dressed in a floor length black gown raised an eyebrow. "Of course."

Pearl started to respond, but remembered she wanted this event to go well for Theo. "Is there a problem?"

"No problem. It's a black tie affair. You are sure to stand out."

"Black tie, you say?" Pearl nodded. "If I remember my etiquette correctly, black tie affairs call for floor length evening gowns, dressy cocktail dresses or an appropriate little black dress. Well, you see, I have these wonderful long legs so why not show them off."

She stuck her leg out to show the woman. The she looked her up and down. "I choose not to look like my ninety-year-old grandmother." She smiled. "Did you find my name?"

The woman nodded her head, clearly offended by Pearl's comment. "Yes," she responded as she stepped aside.

"Snotty heifer," Pearl mumbled as two men dressed in tuxedos opened the double doors to the main ballroom. She glanced around the room. "Well, the Prentiss certainly know how to put on a function."

The room was decorated in ivory and gold. There were no chair covers at this event. No, there were gold chairs with white drapes down the back and tied with gold ribbons. The centerpieces were tall, gold vases with beautiful long stem white roses. The tables were set with gold goblets and flatware. The crystal place settings sparkled where the lights from the chandelier hit them. The place was elegance at its best. Pearl was impressed with the tasteful elegance until she turned to see a blonde a little too close to Theo.

He saw her the moment those legs took the first step into the room. The little black dress caught his attention so completely he lost track of what Amber was saying. The shoulders and sleeves were lace, the bodice hit every curve, the bottom flared, the heels, at least four inches, added more length to those shapely legs of hers. Theo's only thought was about the feel of those legs wrapped around him so possessively last night. His eyes weren't the only ones on Pearl as she walked confidently towards him. All sounds or thoughts of anything else disappeared.

"Excuse me, Dr. Prentiss. May I have a moment?"

Theo never looked away from Pearl. Just as he was about to respond his mother joined them.

"Theo." She kissed him on the cheek. "Well, aren't you going to introduce me to your date?" She turned to the blonde.

Pearl raised an eyebrow as she saw the frown on Theo's face. He turned his mother towards her and Pearl smiled.

"Mother, this is Pearl Lassiter." He stepped closer putting his arm around Pearl's waist. "Pearl, my mother, Leonora Prentiss.

Pearl extended her hand. "Mrs. Prentiss, it's a pleasure to meet you."

Leonora looked from Pearl to the blonde standing to the side. "You're joking?"

Pearl lowered her hand. "Amber works at the hospital. She did not come with me."

"But you've been standing here talking with her. I thought she was with you…with you."

"No, and you are being rude to Pearl."

She turned. "I don't mean to be rude. Of course it's nice to meet you. I just could not fathom you would be here with my son."

"Good evening. Who do we have here?" Theo's father walked up behind his wife and smiled at Pearl.

"Dad, this is Pearl Lassiter. Pearl, my father Edward."

Pearl hesitated to extend her hand and be embarrassed again. She found the action wasn't necessary. Edward walked around his wife, took Pearl's hands and held them out.

"My goodness. If I may say so, I taught my son well. You, my dear, are a goddess. Tell me, can those legs move on a dance floor?"

Pearl smiled at the tall, handsome, dark haired Caucasian with the hazel eyes, and though surprised, many things about him reminded her of Theo. "Yes, they can." She took his hand then smiled over her shoulder at Theo as they walked to the center of the room.

Theo returned the smile until his mother spoke. "I cannot believe you would bring someone like that to my birthday party."

"Like what, Mother?"

"Well..." she stuttered. "Take a look at her." She pointed towards the dance floor. "Look at the dress, it's disgraceful and her hair. My goodness it looks like she didn't bother to comb it."

"I think her hair is beautiful," Amber said from behind them.

Both Theo and Leonora turned and glared at her. Amber looked embarrassed then walked away.

"How could you?"

"How could I what, Mother?" Theo turned his back to the dance floor to ensure Pearl did not see him as he spoke to his mother. "Find someone who's young, vibrant, beautiful and sexy as hell. Look at the men in this room, Mother. They can't take their eyes off of her."

"Because she's dressed like a ... a..."

"Check yourself, Mother. I care for this woman. I suggest you take a moment to carefully determine your next move."

"Theo..."

"Before I walk away, please tell me you are not upset because she is Black."

"I don't have a problem with her being...Black. She's just...so natural."

"Hun hum." Theo walked away joining his father and Pearl on the dance floor.

He took Pearl in his arms, kissed her cheek, then whispered in her ear, "Boy shorts or thong?"

Pearl's laughter rang out. "You know you are in trouble, don't you?"

"I figured as much." He smiled into her eyes.

"You didn't tell your mother about me. You didn't tell me about your father and you forgot to tell me what type of event this was." She leaned in and whispered in his ear, "You want to tell me why you caused this little scene?"

"I honestly did not consider there would be a scene. Did you notice my mother is Black?"

"I did." She smiled. "I also notice she thought you were with a Caucasian. Could it be that is who she is used to seeing with you?"

"It's possible, only because I've never brought many around my parents."

"So I'm a novelty to her."

"No, you're a freaking goddess and you know it. Can I turn you in this dress?"

"And put on a bigger show than we are right now? I don't think so."

"But I so want to see that show," he laughed.

Pearl joined him. "You can turn me when we get back to your place."

Theo kissed her lips. "I can't wait."

Edward took Leonora aside. He waved at the attendees with the curious stares and smiled as he spoke to his wife. He reached into his pocket and pulled out his wallet. On the inside was a picture of his wife. "I want you to take a good look at this picture. Now take a glance at that beautiful young woman with our son. Isn't it a joy to know he loves you so much that he wanted his wife to be just like you?"

"Wife? I think you are putting too much into this, Edward. This is the first time we have even seen her. Why, he's never mentioned her before."

"Yet he brings her to the one event where all of his family and friends are in attendance, including his mother. If that doesn't convince you, I want you to take a look at them on the dance floor. I see magic. What do you see?"

Leonora looked over at her son for a long moment. There was something different about the way he was holding... "What's her name again?"

"Pearl." Edward smiled at his wife.

"Well..." Leonora folded the wallet and put it back in his pocket. "Let's get to know Pearl."

After the ceremony and well wishes were made everyone was seated for a five-course meal. Leonora sat between her husband and Theo. Pearl sat to Theo's right. A few others joined them at the table, including a last minute addition of a woman named Lauren.

"So, Pearl, please tell us about yourself. What do you do for a living?"

Pearl was startled, for the woman had made every effort to keep the conversation flowing without her. She felt Theo's hand on her leg as she looked up at his mother. This is where she had to make a decision. As much as she cared for Theo, she couldn't be anyone other than who she was. "I talk to people for a living."

"That could cover a range of possibilities. Do you work at a grocery store, a movie theater or are you a comedian? When someone asks a question of this nature it's an attempt to get to know you."

Theo started to speak, but Pearl grabbed his hand under the table.

"Pearl is the Press Secretary for Attorney General Harrison," Edward replied before Pearl could.

"Really?" Leonora appeared to be a bit surprised. "How on earth did you meet someone working for that man, Theo?"

"That man?" Pearl questioned. "JD Harrison is one of the youngest Attorney Generals in the country. He was also elected by one of the widest margins in recent history. I think he deserves the respect of being called by his name. If you can't bring yourself to do that, simply call him Mr. Attorney General."

"I actually voted for him," Lauren offered with a shrug of her shoulder. "He's a good man." The redhead nodded to Pearl. "I've seen you at a few press conferences. Very impressive. Did you help with his acceptance speech?"

"The AG likes to write his own speeches, most of the time it's from the hip. We develop a message and pray he stays the course when he speaks."

"Well, whatever you are doing the message is being received."

"By whom, the people who want us to take care of them and highjack our cars if we don't? The only thing I ever hear him talk about is saving gangbangers."

"Mother, it's your birthday, let's find another topic other than criticizing Pearl's employer."

"So, did you go to school to learn to talk to people, Ms. Lassiter?"

"Of course she did," Edward replied. "Master's in Public Administration. I like that, brains and beauty."

"Edward," Leonora interrupted, "let Ms. Lassiter speak for herself."

"Yes, please do." Pearl glared at Leonora. "Was it when I said hello, or the moment you realized your son was with a Black woman that you decided not to like me? Don't get me wrong, the feeling is mutual at this point, but I was wondering what exactly set you off?"

"For one, it was the way you came dressed to a formal event."

"I love that dress," Lauren stated. "Wish I had the legs to wear it."

Pearl smiled. "Thanks, Lauren. How did you get pulled into this?"

"I'm so happy you asked. You see, Leonora feels the more she pushes me in Theo's face, the chance of probability will kick in and we will have sex, marry or do something. What she doesn't know is we tried that and though he was good, we are just not compatible. You on the other hand are a good match for him if for no reason than you will stand up to his mother and her meddling."

Theo laughed as did Pearl. "You thought you were the first smart mouth woman in my life."

"Lauren, I have never seen this side of you," Lenora huffed.

"I know, Mrs. Prentiss, and I'm sorry. Anyone in this room can see there is something special between these two." She wiped her mouth. "I say leave them alone. Let them explore the possibility of finding happiness, just like you did." She stood. "Please excuse me."

"Well, I never knew she was such a liberal."

"You say that as if it's a bad thing." Pearl smiled. "It's a wonderful thing to care about others who happen to be less fortunate than we are."

"Why would I care?" Leonora snapped back. "I depended on me to get my education to raise my status. I did not use affirmative action or student loans to make my way through college. I worked to acquire what we have today, as I expect every other person to do. The one thing I did not do was send my son to college to become a doctor, only to be pulled backwards by an around the way girl with kinky hair and long legs."

"You're a Republican?" Pearl stood with a look of outrage. "How in the hell can you be a Republican in this day and time? Oh, wait." She looked around. "You don't believe there's a struggle going on? You think because you have the wealth and means to do things you consider important, that all doors are opened to you." Pearl leaned across the table into Leonora's face. "Let me enlighten you. My boss is a damn good man. He believes in serving all the people in the commonwealth, including over-opinionated, right wing conservatives such as yourself. As Attorney General he ensures you have the right to drive in any neighborhood without being stopped for driving while Black. You want to know something else, the moment you step outside of your little box and venture into an area above your means, and there are a quite a few, you too will be pulled over and questioned, arrested or possibly killed for the color of your skin." She picked up her purse. "The struggle isn't over. It's just dressed differently. Now, you think about that while you are celebrating the very liberties JD Harrison is trying to protect the next time you want to judge him or me. Oh, and by the way, I love my kinky hair. Can you say the same or are you too busy trying to hide who you truly are with the piece of crap human being you've become?" She didn't bother to wait for a response or Theo to catch up with her. Pearl strolled to the coat checkroom, retrieved her coat and headed towards the valet.

Theo was shell-shocked. He had never heard anyone speak to his mother in that manner. She deserved it, but it had never been delivered in that manner. He stood slowly. "I'm going to check on Pearl. Dad, will you..." His father waved his hand

"Well." Edward stood. "I guess she told you."

"Edward," Leonora huffed.

"Oh come on, Nora. You were egging that young woman on from the moment she arrived." He kissed her on the cheek to soften his rebuff. "I dare to say, you have met your match. Now, come and dance with me so I can seduce you into some birthday loving later tonight before you have to clean up this mess you've created with Theo."

Theo walked out the door and slowed when he saw Pearl waiting for the valet. He stood next to her with his coat over his arm. "Do I still get my dance tonight?"

Pearl looked sideways at him. "Your mother and I will probably never get along."

He took her coat from her and put it on her. "Of course you will. As soon as you both realize you love me as much as the other."

Pearl froze. "I never said that. I never said I love you."

"You did one better. You showed me."

"When and how?"

"Tonight when you stayed after the first insult my mother issued. Then again when you did not hold me accountable for my mother's actions or thoughts."

Pearl just stared at him until the valet pulled up with her car. "Nice car."

"Thank you." She hesitated. "My boyfriend helped me pick it out."

He kissed her. "I'll see you at the condo."

"Don't you think you'd better check on your mother?"

"No." He shook his head. "That is my father's problem to handle tonight. I have my own angry woman to soothe this evening."

Chapter 9

"You do not come into my home to humiliate my daughter." Sally Lassiter was sitting, actually a little excited that Theo's mother had called and asked if she could come by to talk until the woman spoke. That's when all hell broke out.

"Mrs. Lassiter, please hear me out."

"Hear you out? You just called my daughter a gold digger and you want me to hear you degrade her further."

"No, I expect you to listen to reason. You are a mother just like I am. You want the best for Pearl just as I want the best for my son. Look around. I'm offering you a better life, all you have to do is convince your daughter to stay away from Theo."

"I'm not in the habit of interfering in my children's lives. I've raised each of them to be strong, successful individuals. They are capable of deciding who they will allow into their lives and who they will not. Frankly, I'm questioning if Theo is worthy of Pearl after meeting you."

"What's all the yelling about?" Phire asked as she walked in from the kitchen. She placed her book bag on the table and stepped into the living room. "Good afternoon," she said to the woman her mother was clearly angry with. She kissed her mother on the cheek.

"Good afternoon." Leonora saw the cheerleading short skirt. "Do all of your girls walk around so barely clothed?"

"What did cheerleaders wear in your day, long gowns and potato sacks?" Phire shot back.

"Mind your manners," Sally reprimanded. "Mrs. Prentiss." Sally sat down and tried to calm down. "What exactly do you have against Pearl?"

"Well for one, she is very opinionated. She lacks manners and she doesn't respect people above her as she should."

"Above her?" Phire questioned. "Who is above her? You?"

"Of course I am." Leonora flipped her hair over her shoulder.

"Pearl Lassiter is not below anyone." The voice came from the stairs behind them. "She is top rated in my book, Mrs. Prentiss," Cynthia Thornton said as she walked into the room in a robe.

"Cynthia, sit before I have to kill that son of mine." Sally helped her to the opposite sofa from Leonora.

"Cynthia, what on earth are you doing here?"

"Recuperating with my soon to be mother-in-law. Why are you here? And please don't tell me it's to protect Theo. Theo will be the first to let you know he's a big boy and can make his own decisions. In fact, I called him to let him know you were here when you arrived. I'm certain he will be knocking on the door soon."

Leonora looked out the window. "Why would you do something like that? Theo did not have to know about this."

"Mrs. Prentiss, I just went through this battle with my mother. I'm debating on inviting her to my wedding. Theo is your only child. Don't put him in that position."

"Theo is not considering marrying that woman."

"Oh, but he is not far from it," Theo said from the doorway. He looked around. "Please tell me Pearl is not here."

"No." Sally stood and walked to Joe who was standing behind Theo.

He put his arms around his wife. "Theo and I met for lunch. He had something he wanted to talk with me about."

Theo walked into the room. He checked Cynthia's pulse then stood. "I don't want your pressure rising. You understand?"

"Yes, Doctor, but you are not here for me." Cynthia stood. "You need to speak to your mother before Phire beats her down for talking about her sister."

"Damn right." Phire rolled her eyes at the woman sitting on the sofa. "Cynthia, I'll help you back upstairs."

Theo took Cynthia's seat and simply stared at his mother. "Why?"

"Because it's been five days and you haven't so much as called to apologize for leaving my birthday party with that woman."

"Her name is Pearl and you might as well get used to it." He got up then sat next to his mother. He took her hand in his. "You told me once, you would have moved heaven and earth to be with Dad. I need you to understand, that's how I feel about Pearl."

Leonora shook her head. "Theo, you are making a mistake."

"That's what Dad's parents said about you." He raised an eyebrow as he spoke to her. "Dad and I had a long talk after your party. He told me how you two had to battle and finally walk away from his family because they felt you were beneath their son. Thank God, Dad did not listen to them. He married you despite his family's protests, despite him losing his trust fund, despite them threatening to have you arrested." He kissed his mother's hand. "I love you and I love Pearl. Please don't make me choose between the two of you."

Leonora stood. "You say you love her. Does she love you?" She put her gloves on and buttoned her coat. "I won't make you choose, son. I'll support whatever you decide to do." She looked around. "I didn't raise you to go backwards. This neighborhood, and this house is not what you are accustomed to."

"Mrs. Prentiss, I understand you are upset with all of this. However, you have insulted my daughter and my home. Now before I put you out I'm going to say this to you once. This house is a home that was built on love and God's grace. All of my children are kind, loving, and caring human beings. One day Pearl will learn of this and will forgive you. As for me, you are not welcome in my home and if I ever hear of you bad mouthing my child again, it will be me who gets arrested."

Joe opened the door for Leonora. "You have a good day, Mrs. Prentiss."

Leonora looked up at him, then to Sally and lastly Theo. "That woman is going to break your heart."

Theo stood as his mother walked out the door. He stopped before leaving. "My apologies for my mother."

Joe hit Theo on the shoulder. "You don't have to apologize, son. You are welcome here, anytime."

"Theo." Sally stepped up and kissed him on the cheek. "This isn't going to be easy for you. If you need to talk, don't hesitate to call."

"Thank you both." Theo exhaled then followed his mother out the door.

Chapter 10

Christmas dinner at the Lassiters was a special time of the year. This was the day that everyone moved heaven and earth to be together. The kitchen was humming with different aromas from the turkey, ham, lasagna, macaroni and cheese, yams, smooth kale salad, potato salad, rice pudding, pound cakes, sweet potato pies, coconut pies, apple pies, German Chocolate Cake and everyone's favorite, hot homemade buttered rolls. Yes, this is the day everyone had a place at the dinner table.

This year there was an extra body in the mix. Cynthia was in the dining room decorating the table when Pearl walked in. She took a look around, to see what Cynthia was doing, then picked up the silverware to help.

"I heard what you said to Theo's mother about me," she began. "Did you mean that?"

Cynthia smiled at the centerpiece she'd just arranged. "Damn I'm good. Look at that."

"I don't think you need me to boost your ego."

"No, I don't. And yes, I meant every word of what I said." Cynthia stopped and looked at her. "Theo is lucky he found you, Pearl. But you don't see it...not yet."

"How do you know what I see," Pearl hissed.

Cynthia sat in one of the chairs at the table. "You are testing him because of what happened in high school. You want him to prove over and over and over that he will never leave. You are fortunate because Theo is the kind that will never leave, no matter what you put him through. He's like Sammy. He found what he wants and he will not let anything come between the two of you. Not even his mother."

"His mother. That heifer can kiss where the sun don't shine."

"How do you think that makes him feel during this, the holiday season? Have you once given any thoughts to what is happening to his heart that he opened to you and had to close to his mother."

"I did not put him in that position, she did."

"Yes, she did but you have the power to correct what she has done. It's a magical time of the year. This is when you do everything in your power to make others' wishes come true. What do you think Leonora Prentiss' wish is today? I'm pretty sure it's to see her only child for Christmas. Do you have enough love in your heart for Theo to make sure that happens? Think about it."

"Why do you care one way or another what happens with his mother?"

"I don't. I care what happens with you." Cynthia stood. "I'm going to see if I can help in the kitchen."

Pearl laughed out loud. Cynthia turned and glared at her. "Sorry, but didn't Tracy, Ashley and Roz put you out of their kitchens?"

"That was before your brother taught me how to cook." Cynthia laughed as she walked out of the room.

"We are talking food, Cynthia, not in the bedroom." Pearl smiled but Cynthia's words were tugging at her heart. Did she love Theo? What would she do if she had to choose between him and her family? "Ha, my family, of course," she said aloud. Then she started to slowly walk towards the kitchen. Looking in, there were all her sisters, her mother and Cynthia. No one should have to choose between someone they love and their family.

"Mom, I'm going to run to the hospital for a minute. I'll be back in time for dinner." Pearl grabbed her coat and ran out the back door.

"Your talk worked." Sally smiled at Cynthia.

"We're going to make you a Lassiter, yet." Phire turned back to the potatoes she was peeling as she spoke to her mother. "You know if we keep going at this rate we will eventually have six daughters-in-law and six sons-in law. That's twelve additional people to the clan you already have." She looked directly at her mother. "Where in the hell are you going to put all those people?"

Pearl went to the reception desk in the emergency room where Theo volunteered for the Christmas shift so those with families could spend the holiday at home. It was the noble thing to do, however, she really would have loved spending Christmas Eve with him.

"Hi, I'm looking for Dr. Theodore Prentiss. Could you tell me where I can find him?"

The nurse looked at the board. "He's in pediatrics. Down the hall, to your right. Can't miss it."

Pearl followed the directions and came to a set of double doors with windows. Through the window she could see Theo sitting in the center of the room surrounded by children. Some were seated on the floor, some in wheelchairs, some in beds. His back was to her when she stepped inside the doors. He was reading The Night Before Christmas to them. Nurses were acting out the characters as he read. The children were smiling. It made her sad. No child should spend Christmas in a hospital.

"Are you here for one of the children?" one of the nurses looked up and asked.

Theo turned to see her and their eyes met. "I'm here for the big child in the center."

"Dr. Theo."

"Ohhhh," the children laughed.

"Would you take over here for a minute?" Theo asked the nurse. He guided Pearl out the room. "Hey." He pulled her to him and kissed her hello. "Merry Christmas."

"Merry Christmas to you."

"Isn't your family about to sit down for dinner?"

She nodded. "In a little bit. You're good with them."

"I enjoy being around them. I love children. I hope to have a boat load one day."

"I haven't thought about children. Never thought I'd have a boyfriend in my life either. I guess I'll have to think about it. But not now."

Theo smiled. "I think you should think about it."

"Theo, I know we're going to meet at your place tonight, but would you do me a favor before we meet?"

"Seems serious."

"It is. Very important to me."

"Anything." Theo pulled her close. "What is it?"

"Would you stop in to see your mother? You're her only child and it's Christmas. Magical things happen at Christmas." A tear ran down her cheek.

"After the way my mother treated you, you're asking me to forgive her."

"I'm not good at this so let me say this without interruption."

"Okay." Theo nodded, then leaned back against the wall.

Pearl exhaled. "I've been single for a long time. It's an adjustment for me to think of someone else in my planning. You've grown on me fast and I'm trying to catch up with you. I'm opening my heart to you and it's scary as hell." She gave a nervous giggle. "The one thing I know is I couldn't make a choice of you in my life or my family. No one should have to make that choice. What your mother did, was out of love for you." She gave him a package. "Wish your parents a Merry Christmas for me."

The plan was already in place, but this sealed it for Theo. This woman gave him the gift of Christmas... love. She didn't say the word, but the sentiment was there. Theo took her in his arms, and kissed her with all the passion and love he had in his heart for her. "Thank you." He took the package. "Is anything in here for me?"

Pearl smiled as she stepped away. "No, your gift comes later."

Pearl made it back to the house just in time to hear Joshua say grace for dinner.

"Lord, we're going to hell for this," Phire giggled.

"If I have to speak to you about your language one more time, young lady, you are going to see the backside of my hand," Sally warned.

"When was the last time Mother spanked any of us?" Luke asked.

"There's a first time for everything," Joe replied to his NFL running back son.

Mathew and Timothy laughed.

"The next person to crack a joke before Joshua can say grace is going to have to deal with me." Samuel looked around the room to ensure he had everyone's attention. With that he looked at Joshua and nodded. "You have the floor."

"Heavenly Father, we come to you asking for your continued grace, mercy, protection and blessings as a family. For all the gifts given and received on this day are in your name. Second Corinthians 9:15: Thanks be to God for his inexpressible gift. That is the gift of life, love and family. As a family we ask together..." The entire family recited the Lord's Prayer:

> "Our Father, which art in heaven,
> Hallowed be thy Name.
> Thy Kingdom come. Thy will be done on earth, as it is in heaven.
> Give us this day our daily bread. And forgive us our trespasses,
> As we forgive them that trespass against us.
> And lead us not into temptation, but deliver us from evil.
> For thine is the kingdom, the power, and the glory, for ever and ever. Amen."

At the conclusion of Joshua's blessing Joe stood with his wine goblet in his hand. "Before we start dinner, your mother and I have something to say."

"Please tell me you're not pregnant," Phire said with a shake of her head. Everyone looked at her, exasperated. "Hey, none of you are around here when they be going at it like rabbits. Y'all don't know. It's a possibility."

"Phire." Sally scowled. "The corner."

"The corner? Mommy, I'm sixteen years old."

"Do you want to see seventeen?" Joe asked.

Phire pushed her chair back from the table and carried it to the corner as her older brothers and sisters looked on.

Joe held his glass high. "I would like to make a toast to welcome Cynthia to our family. With open arms and hearts we thank you for bringing love into Samuel's life."

"To Samuel and Cynthia," Sally joined in. "May your love bring you children to love and happiness throughout."

"Here, here," Ruby added and raised her glass as they all toasted the new couple.

Pearl gave Phire a sad smile. "Mother, can Phire come back to the table. She promises to be quiet?"

Sally looked over at her youngest.

"It's Christmas," Jade added.

"It is, Mother," Adam added. "I'll seal her mouth with a special tape I developed if she gets out of line."

"Are all of you going to badger me until I say yes?"

"Yes," the family replied in unison.

They all looked at Sally and waited. "One word, young lady, and it's upstairs the next time."

Phire quickly put her chair back at the table.

Samuel stood with Cynthia at his side. "Family is what brings us together. Love is what binds us. Thank you for accepting Cynthia." His eyes went to Pearl. "We want you all to be the first to know we set our wedding date for February 14th."

Everyone cheered. "Congratulations."

"Are there anymore announcements?" Mathew asked. "I'm ready to eat."

"Then let's dig in," Joe stated as he began carving the turkey.

Theo entered his parents' home knowing they would be in the great room having an after dinner sherry before they opened gifts. His father was the first to see him.

Edward stood. "You're a good son. Merry Christmas." He walked over to hug Theo. Leonora stood with tears on the brim of her eyelids. "Does this mean you've come to your senses?"

Theo and Edward shared a look, before he walked over to her. He hugged his mother. "Merry Christmas, Mother." He gave her a large red bag and a box wrapped in gold. "This is from Pearl."

Leonora jumped back as if the box could bite her. Theo put his hand up. "Why don't we have a seat before you say something that will cause me to leave? Can we do that?"

Leonora nodded and exhaled. "Is there a bomb in the box?"

Theo put his coat on the back of the chair, then took a seat. "I don't have long, I'm on call at the hospital until midnight."

"You volunteered again this year," Edward asked.

"You weren't invited to that house for dinner?"

Theo sat back. "Let's talk about that house and the family who lives there or used to live there. I think it's important for us to move past this as a family. Joe and Sally Lassiter have twelve children."

"That's not surprising. All people like them do is have babies and expect others to take care of them."

"Leonora, I strongly urge you to let Theo have his say before you lose your son for good."

Leonora crossed her legs and nodded. "I'm sorry, Theo. Please continue."

"Of the twelve children, all have attended college or are currently attending with the exception of the youngest daughter. To attend school each child with a job helped the next child with tuition. The Lassiters pay for their own. They don't ask anyone for anything. When one purchases a new car the old car goes to the next in line. Another amazing fact about that family is the success of their children. The oldest was a Navy Seal, next in line manages Vital Records for the state, the next works for the CIA, Pearl is the press secretary for the Attorney General and a man very likely to be President one day. You talk about these people being beneath us when the fact is we are nowhere in their class." He sat forward. "You want to know the reason

I'm here tonight? Pearl asked me to come. She said no one should be put in a place to have to choose between a love and their family. You put me in that position. And I have to be honest, I couldn't walk away from Pearl now to save my life. I love you, Mother. But Pearl is going to be my future. I'm not saying today or tomorrow, but have no doubt she will be there. The question now is, will you?" He stood and kissed his mother on the cheek. "I pray you will." He put his coat on, then shook his father's hand. "I love you, Dad. I'll talk with both of you tomorrow." Theo turned and walked out of the house.

Pearl was waiting in the parking lot when Theo pulled up a little after midnight. He grabbed her hand and ran to the elevator. "I have a surprise for you."

"You do," she laughed as they ran.

"I do," he said as he kissed her passionately while the elevator car traveled upwards. "I've wanted to do that ever since you left the hospital."

"Hmm," she moaned. "I've been wanting to do this since I met you." She unbuttoned her coat. Underneath she was wrapped in nothing but red ribbon with a big bow across her breasts. "Merry Christmas, baby. BAM!"

Theo's eyes sparkled as the elevator came to a stop. He quickly pulled her coat over her as one of his neighbors entered.

"Hope you have a happy holiday, Dr. Prentiss." The man nodded.

"It's beginning to look a lot like Christmas," was all Theo could say. As they stepped off the elevator Pearl turned to the man and in the sweetest voice said, "Merry Christmas."

Theo quickly opened the door and ravished her as they fell to the floor laughing. "I love you, Pearl Lassiter." He kissed her again, then used his teeth to unwrap his present, his lips to wish her a Merry Christmas and his tongue to welcome in the New Year. Both were naked and it was an hour later when they made it to her present.

Theo held his hand out to help her up. "Close your eyes. I have to give you my present."

Pearl laughed, "I thought I just received my present."

Theo smiled. "I have more. Close your eyes."

"I hate surprises."

"You'll love this one," he said as he helped her up. "Are your eyes closed?'

"Yes, yes, what is it?"

He put her in the center of the entrance to the living room. "Open your eyes."

Pearl opened her eyes to see the living room was completely furnished. Not just furniture, but the exact pieces placed where she said a few weeks earlier. There was a long sofa and ottoman, no table facing the fireplace. A Persian carpet lay between the two. She then walked towards the windows to find a chaise lounge with a table next to it on the other side of the Christmas tree.

"Theo." She shook her head and laughed. "It's beautiful. It is simply stunning." She looked around at the paintings hung on the wall and could not believe he took her literally.

"I want you to feel at home every time you walk in the door." He took the blanket that was on the back of the sofa and placed it on the floor in front of the tree. "Sit." He went into the kitchen and brought back a tray with grapes and cheese, two wine glasses and a bottle of red wine, then sat on the floor next to her. "Open this present first." He gave her a small red box.

"Theo, you've given enough."

"We are going to open every one of these boxes. I want to know what's inside those." He pointed to the boxes she'd put under the tree.

"You are worse than a kid at Christmas."

"I know, now open this."

"Okay, okay." Pearl unwrapped the box, then opened it. Inside was a key. "What is it to?"

"Here." He held her eyes. "I want you to know you are the only one I will be seeing. If I thought you wouldn't turn me down I would be asking you to marry me, Pearl Lassiter, for I am hopelessly in love with you. I don't see it changing, or altering in any way. If I wasn't certain before, I was sure the moment you insisted I talk to my mother." He shook his head at the thought. "The hell with it, I'm asking any way. Pearl Lassiter, will you marry me?"

"Theo." Pearl inhaled then closed her eyes. When she opened them, she moved closer to him. "I'm going to say no with a qualifier. I am so sure I'm in love with you too. The thought of you not being in my life hit me earlier today. It is not something I want to endure. But I'm damaged material, Theo, and you deserve better. I can be that better, I'm just not there yet. Will you wait for me to be the best Pearl I can be and ask me again? Please?"

He kissed her so tenderly her heart melted. "That was the sweetest rejection I have ever heard."

They both laughed as they kissed. "I'll wait forever for you, Pearl. But I have no issues with the Pearl you are now. I know you do, but I love you as you are."

She kissed his face all over. "Thank you, thank you, thank you."

Chapter 11
Six Years Later

"Why are we having this argument again?" Pearl threw her hands in the air. "We just won a freakin' Presidential Election. There is a hell of a celebration going on out there. Why are we in here?"

Theo was thrilled for her. She was about to become the Press Secretary for the President of the United States. Pride filled him in a way he would never be able to express. However, a fear consumed him. He was about to lose her. This meant she would be moving to DC. No, it wasn't far away; however, it wasn't right across town either.

"Theo?"

"Six years ago I asked you to marry me. You said you had this thing to do." He took a step towards her with his hand out. She took it. "You've done it, Pearl." He pulled out a blue velvet box, then bent down on one knee. He opened the box, then looked up at her. "I'm asking again. Will you marry me?"

Pearl could not take her eyes from the ring. It was a platinum ring with a diamond cluster holding a pearl in the center.

"You see, you are the center of my universe. I don't want to imagine a day without you in my life."

She got down on her knees. "I love you and want to spend the rest of my life with you." She kissed his cheek, then closed the lid on the box. "Babe, we talked about this. This is the super bowl of my career. We're about to make history here."

"That's not more important than our life together, Pearl."

"Yes, Theo. At this moment it is. We have an opportunity to make the lives of everyone in this country better, safer. That is bigger than the two of us. We can wait a little longer."

The kiss they shared was deep, searing, loving. So much so, Pearl felt something else. She felt finality in the kiss.

Theo ended the kiss, holding her face cupped in the palms of his hands as he stared into her eyes. "Nothing in this life is more important to me than you." He stood bringing her up with him. He held her hands, then brought them to his lips and kissed them "You have to take moments, for tomorrow is not promised to anyone, Pearl."

There was a knock on the door. "Pearl, the President-elect is about to take the stage. He wants you there."

Pearl hesitated. "Theo…"

"Go." He kissed her forehead. "You don't want to keep the country waiting."

There was something in his stance that told her not to leave. There was another knock on the door, this time accompanied with cheers of victory.

"We did it," the voices rang out.

Pearl looked towards the door. Theo stepped away. He smiled, then nodded his head. "Go celebrate your victory."

"Come with me."

"No, this is the team's moment. You go ahead."

She picked up her hotel door key. "You'll be out soon, right?"

"Yes. I'll be out."

Pearl smiled, then walked out the door.

The red flirty dress swinging around those beautiful legs as she walked out the door remained with Theo as he packed his bag. Their plan was to stay at the hotel to be a part of the celebration. While he was ecstatic for her, he didn't feel much like celebrating.

After six years of supporting, encouraging and loving her, Pearl did not see the future with them as husband and wife. She did not see that they could have both. Now, it would be more difficult. They would have to deal with putting together a transition team to hire a White House staff. Her days would be filled with press conferences and speech writing. He smiled with pride knowing she would excel in her new role as The White House Press Secretary. How could he compete with that? What made him think being Mrs. Theodore Prentiss would ever compare? He slowly eased into his leather jacket, put his overnight bag on his shoulder. He looked around the room as he put his hand in his pocket. He closed his eyes as his fingers touched the blue velvet box. Pulling it out, he exhaled. The five-karat diamond setting had cost a small fortune. The pearl in the center had been shipped from the Persian Gulf. It doubled the cost of the diamonds surrounding it. He opened the box. The ring was as precious and as beautiful as the woman he had it designed for. No one would ever be able to wear it but her. He closed the box, placed it on top of her tablet, which she rarely parted from, then turned and walked out of the door.

Theo had reached the lobby of the hotel that was filled with news reporters with microphones, posed in front of cameras all talking at the same time. Crowds of people were everywhere as he made his way to the front door. He gave his claim ticket to the valet. People were rushing through, trying to join the celebration inside, as he waited for his car to be brought around. All he could do was smile at the eager faces. The hope and excitement in everyone who entered the building was contagious. But it all evaded him. His hope exited when Pearl walked out of the room.

"Here you are, Dr. Prentiss." The valet gave Theo his keys as he received his tip. "What a shame to get called away on this historical night. You're going to miss...."

Gunfire rang out. The valet and Theo turned to see people screaming, running from the ballroom. Gunshots exploded again as now crowds poured stumbling on top of each other towards the door. Police officers and agents ran towards the room. Theo threw his bag in the backseat of his car then pulled a medical bag from the trunk of the car. He ran back into the hotel, pushing his way through the crowd. Some of the faces were recognizable; others were not as the crowd grew in numbers in the lobby. By the time he reached the ballroom, the area was almost empty. Bodies were on the floor, some injured, some he was certain were dead. He looked towards the stage to see JD and Tracy on the floor next to one of the children. Agents surrounded them as Tracy's screams drowned out the other moans and yells that filled the room.

"Pearl?" he whispered to himself as he looked franticly around.

"Theo!"

He heard someone call his name. "Theo, we need a doctor up here."

Theo looked up to see Brian motioning to him to come forward. "Where's Pearl?"

"I don't known, man. Get up here. JC was hit."

Theo ran to the stage as Brian shouted to get the President-elect out of the room. Theo immediately went to work on the young boy, who the agents were trying to pry from his mother's arms.

"Tracy." Theo took her hands. "Let me look at JC, please. I can help him." He then looked at JD who was not much better off than his wife. "JD," Theo pleaded.

JD took Tracy in his arms and Theo went to work on stabilizing the young boy. The paramedics arrived just as he saw Pearl enter the room from the side door.

Relief washed over him as he continued to work on JC. Once the child was stabilized he handed him over to the EMTs then went to the next body on the stage. The next few hours were filled with treatment of gunshot wounds, crushed hands, concussions and unfortunately, the pronouncements of deaths. Hours later he was in the hospital saving as many lives as he could.

Pearl went to work organizing the care efforts. For the next few hours it was taking names, getting information from EMTs, the hospital then reporting the happenings to the reporters. The night of victory had turned into one of violence and despair. For hours, the police, Secret Service officers and others tried to piece together all that had happened as Pearl gathered information to inform families of the condition of loved ones. She had spoken to her parents to ensure them, she, Samuel and Joshua were fine and working the scene. She had even spoken to Theo's parents to let them know Theo was not injured. She had seen him and knew he was in surgery working on patients, but they had not had a chance to talk. Her heart, her body, her everything longed to talk with him, touch him, hold him. Now, she sat in the corner of the hospital waiting room, with others, waiting for news on loved ones. She turned towards the wall and pulled out the blue velvet box.

Earlier, which seemed like decades ago now, she had reached the ballroom and spoke with JD. He and Tracy were in the VIP lounge, now surrounded by more Secret Service Agents than before. All of the staff as well as family members and friends were there with them. She gave him his speech and watched as he reviewed it. In truth it was all his own words. That's the type of man he was and the kind of President the citizens of the United States would get in his new role. With all the pride she had in the President-elect, he was not the man in the forefront of her mind.

"This looks good, Pearl," JD said as he scanned through the document.

Pearl reached for the document. "I'll have it placed in the teleprompter, Mr. President-elect."

"It's still JD."

"No, Sir," Pearl corrected. "It's not and it will not be for the rest of your life. You will be referred to as Mr. President. Get used to it."

"Not to my family and friends," JD corrected as he hugged her. "You ready to be Press Secretary?"

Pearl beamed with glee, ready to answer but she held back. "Pearl?"

"I'm ready to serve at the will of the President."

JD nodded. "Good." Then he looked around the room. "Could I have everyone's attention for a moment?"

"You have our attention for the next four years," someone replied causing the room to erupt into cheers.

Tracy pulled Pearl aside as JD talked to the group. "Is everything okay?"

Pearl nodded. "You ever wonder what life would be like without JD?"

"Not in the last ten years, no. Before that I fully expected him to be out of my life by now."

"But he's still here."

"Yes, he is," Tracy replied as she took Pearl's hand. "Love enhances accomplishing something as wonderful as this. Having that special someone in your life to share these moments is a blessing. It's not easy to find that one person who will put up with all our little inner demons and stay by our side year after year after year. I tell you, Pearl, both of us are blessed to have a very special man in our life."

"Tracy." JD held out his hand to her.

"Excuse me, The President is calling," she giggled.

Pearl smiled as she watched the two hold hands as JD talked. Flashes of Theo in the room, standing near the fireplace with that look of longing in his eyes hit her like a ton of bricks. "He's leaving," she whispered to herself. As the reality hit her she began backing out of the room. As soon as the door closed behind her, Pearl ran to the elevator and pushed the button. It was on the ninth floor. She looked around and ran to the stairwell. She ran to the fourth floor non-stop then burst into the room. It was as she suspected...empty. "Theo," she called out to the empty sitting room, then ran to the bedroom. His bag was gone. All signs of him were gone.

She backed out of the room shaking her head. "This is not happening, not tonight." She walked back into the sitting area, grabbed her coat and purse. That's when she saw the blue box sitting on top of her tablet on the table. She dropped everything as tears began to stream down her face. She picked up the box, opened it and stared at the beautiful ring inside.

She stared at the ring now, as she was surrounded by cries of relief and some of sadness as news about victims slowly came. *'You have to take moments, for tomorrow isn't promised to anyone.'* Pearl closed the box, wiped a tear from her cheek. She walked over to the nurse's station.

"Excuse me, could you tell me if Dr. Prentiss is still in surgery?"

"It's going to be a few more hours."

"I'll wait for him. Please let him know I'm here as soon as he finishes up."

"I will, Ms. Lassiter. You could wait for him in the lounge. It may be a little more comfortable."

"Thank you."

It was three hours later. Pearl had completed two press conferences, written a response from the President-Elect about the death of the Vice-President Elect and a status update on the condition of Carolyn Roth-Roberts, the Governor's wife. She also checked on the status of the President-Elect's son, who had been shot as well. The next few days which should have been filled with celebrations was now forever marred in their minds. It was now Pearl's job to help the country through this act of terror. Before she could do that, she had to see Theo. She had to tell him yes, she would marry him. This night proved his words to be true, tomorrow is not promised.

It was well after four in the morning and Theo was still in surgery. Pearl could not keep her eyes open any longer. She put her purse under her head, her coat over her body, then curled up in a chair in the lounge and closed her eyes. A few hours later she awakened to sounds of activity in the lounge and wrapped in Theo's arms. She was so relieved to feel him next to her tears sprang to her eyes.

She wrapped her arms around his waist, kissed his cheek then laid back down on his shoulder. "I love you, Theo."

Theo turned towards her, tightened his hold, kissed her forehead, and yawned, "I love you, too." They both fell back to sleep, but not for long.

"Dr. Prentiss, wake up." A nurse shook his shoulder. "Dr. Prentiss."

"Yes." Theo sprang up.

"There's been a complication with Mrs. Roberts. You're needed."

Before Theo could register the statement, there was another burst through the door.

"Pearl." James appeared. "You're needed."

They moved as quickly as they could, and just like that were off to the demands of their careers. Neither had a chance to express their feelings from the night before.

The next few weeks were hectic. The transition team was formed and Pearl's job was to keep the public and the media abreast of all the changes. The aftermath of the shooting and the investigation that followed only added to her tasks. Her time was now being spent between Richmond and Washington, leaving little time for Theo.

Theo, in turn, kept busy at the hospital, volunteering for extra shifts and rotations for other physicians. He also spent more hours at his medical outreach clinic where he gave free medical services, no questions asked to high-risk communities. He did anything to keep from thinking about the state of his relationship with Pearl. He loved her beyond reason. He wanted a family and the rest of his life with her. However, she did not want the same. For weeks he had been trying to sort through his feelings about that. The reality was this would be JD Harrison's first term in office. If he decided to run for re-election that would be a total of eight more years he would have to play second fiddle to Pearl's career. He was thirty-six, she was now thirty-two. If they were going to have a family the time was now, not eight years from now. The question for him was simple. Did he surrender, lick his wounds and find someone else to have a family and life with or did he remain with Pearl knowing he would always come second to her career? It was a difficult decision and one he avoided.

Chapter 12

In the six years they had been dating, Theo had not missed a Thanksgiving dinner. His presence was missed this year, not only at the table, but also on the football field and the roof, where lights needed to be hung for the holidays. However, that was not the clincher for Pearl.

The clincher was a week later while pouring through requests for tickets to the Presidential Inauguration. Each person had to be vetted or investigated before acceptance or denial. Those moving to the level of possible acceptance appeared on a list for Pearl to do a media search for anything that may reflect poorly on the President-Elect. It was during the search she ran across a picture of Theo with Martin Burke, the man seeking tickets. Pearl read the article to find Dr. Burke was presenting the Humanitarian Award honoring Theodore J. Prentiss for his extraordinary work with the community. It was one of the highest honors in the medical profession.

The ceremony had taken place last Saturday in Richmond. Theo was accepting the award dressed in his tuxedo, looking fine as ever. There was something about the picture that caught Pearl as being sad. He was smiling and according to the article he said all the right things, including thank his parents and everyone who supported him in the quest to build the free medical clinic. He should be thrilled at the honor at such a young age. His handsome smile lit up the page; however, his eyes told a different story. They were sad.

Why didn't she know about this? He never mentioned it to her. They had talked several times over the last weeks and he never mentioned the ceremony or that he was being honored. Yes, they had been busy and hadn't had much time for anything, but this was important to him. She knew it was. So why hadn't he shared it with her?

Pearl sat back and thought. Had he mentioned it and she forgot? Had he asked and she turned him down? Her heart began to pound a little harder inside her chest. The more she thought back, she was certain he had not mentioned this to her. Now she was angry. How could he not want her to be a part of something so monumental in his life? She picked up her cell phone and dialed his number.

"Hey." His voice always made her heart sing.

"Hey yourself," Theo replied. "Are you in Richmond or DC?"

"In DC at the transition office." She sat up. "I just came across a very handsome picture of you."

"I have a number of them around, you know."

She smiled. "Ha ha. No, this one was taken on Saturday where you were honored. Why didn't you tell me about this?" There was silence on the other end. An uneasy feeling came over her.

"I didn't think my ego could take another blow."

"Theo." Her heart pounding increased. "I don't understand."

"You are busy right now with everything that's happening. I didn't want you to have to choose. To be honest, I didn't know if I would be on the short end of that decision." There was a sound in the background. "I have to go the nurse's station is calling."

"Theo, I love you."

"I know you do. We'll talk later." With that the call was disconnected and he was gone.

For a long moment Pearl stared at her phone. She was still in that state when Christine knocked on her opened door.

"The President-Elect wants to know if you have the draft on his decision for Vice-President?"

Pearl reached for the paper sitting on the corner of her desk and gave it to Christine.

"Are you okay?"

Pearl looked up. "Sure." Then she looked back at the phone. "I'm fine." But she wasn't. She had that same feeling that hit her stomach the night of the shooting when she found Theo's things gone from the hotel room. Things still weren't right and her world was off center.

"You know he is going to have questions. Are you coming?"

***

The moment Sally saw her daughter get out of her car she knew something was wrong. It was difficult not to notice Theo hadn't been around for a few weeks. Pearl indicated he was busy, but she knew better.

"Time for some tough love." Sally wiped her hands on the dishtowel, opened the back door and held her arms out for her daughter with no clue.

"Mommy." Pearl walked right into her mother's arms and cried. "I don't know how to fix this. I don't want to lose him, Mommy. I love him so much. I can't imagine my life without him in it."

Sally held Pearl at arm's length. The tears in her daughter's eyes tore at her heart. "Have you told him that, Pearl, or have you been too busy telling him to jump and how high to jump to tell him how you feel about him?"

"Mommy?"

"Don't Mommy me." She took her daughter by the hand. "Have a seat. Let me school you before you let that piss ass boy from high school ruin the rest of your life." Sally reached into the cabinet, pulled out a bottle of rum, then a can of coke from the refrigerator. "I'm surprised Theo has stayed around as long as he has." She poured a glass of rum and coke for Pearl and then one for herself. "He has jumped through every hoop you have thrown his way. Yet you keep raising it higher. Drink." She took a drink and waited for Pearl to do the same.

"Um, Mommy, I don't need a lecture. I need you to tell me how to fix this."

"You are right, you don't need a lecture, you need a good old fashioned butt whipping for making Theo wait this long. I've watched your relationship over the years. And I can't believe I raised a child as selfish as you. Every year Theo gives up his family to spend the holidays with you; not once in six years have you spent any holidays with his family, nor have you invited them to spend the holidays with us. Everything has been on your terms. How many ways can the man prove he loves you? He is not going anywhere. Or is that it, Pearl? You know he's not going anywhere so you keep pushing him to the side for your career. Here's something you need to know, little lady. Love is a two way street. You have to give love to receive love. And if you don't get that chip off your shoulder and stop making Theo pay for a little boy's actions, you are not going to ever have room in your heart for anyone. You might as well let Theo go so he can find someone who will give him a family and love him the way he deserves to be loved." She poured another drink in Pearl's glass. "Drink."

Sally watched the tears stream down Pearl's face.

She took her daughter's hand. "Do you truly love him, Pearl?"

Pearl nodded her head. "Yes," she replied with a hiccup. "So much it hurts."

"Good."

"You said love isn't supposed to hurt."

"When you're being stupid it does."

They both laughed. Pearl sniffled. "Mommy, tell me what to do."

"I can't tell you that. You have to look into your heart to find the answers." She patted Pearl's hand. "Christmas is coming. It's always a magical time. Make this a Christmas about Theo. Show him how much you do care."

Pearl was a bit tipsy by the time her mother finished with her. Instead of driving home, she went up to her old bedroom and fell across the bed. Between the tears and rum, she was out of it in a matter of minutes.

Sally took the opportunity to call Theo. He arrived within the hour. She pulled down another glass, filled it with rum and coke and pointed. "Drink."

"Um, Mrs. Lassiter, I am on call."

"Not tonight. As many hours as you've pulled someone can take this shift for you. Drink and then make the call." Theo did as he was instructed.

"How old are you, Theo?"

"Excuse me?"

"I did not stammer, Theodore. How old are you?"

"Thirty-six."

"That's about what I thought." Sally took a drink. "Plan on having a family?"

Theo took a drink then exhaled. "Where is this going, Mrs. Lassiter?"

"Theodore, I asked you a question."

Theo nodded. "Yes, ma'am, I do."

"You plan on having it with someone other than Pearl?"

"That wasn't in my plan."

"Is it in your plans now? Is there someone else in your life?"

"No, there is no one else in my life. I wouldn't do that to Pearl."

"Why the hell not?" Sally took a drink. "The woman has had you kiss her behind for six years. Six years, Theo. When is enough...enough? You are supposed to be the man in that relationship, not Pearl. Your career is just as, if not more demanding, than hers. With the outcome of the election, that is going to change. Her life will not be her own. She is going to be one of the most recognized women in the country. How are you going to give me grandchildren, if you two don't make the time to have sex?"

Theo eyed the woman he had come to love like a mother, then looked at the almost empty bottle of rum. One hundred and fifty proof Jamaican rum. He moved the bottle out of her reach.

"I want you to hear me out. Please don't be offended, for what I'm about to say is from the heart. I love you like one of my own. I think you know that. But you are one of the biggest fools I have ever come across. You are clearly in love with her and she is in love with you. You've allowed her to do things her way long enough. Marry the woman."

Theo wanted to scream, that's what he had been trying to do. But he could see Mrs. Lassiter was in no condition to hear him. "Where is Pearl?"

Sally wiped her brow. "Upstairs in her room. She couldn't hang. Whew." She began to fan herself. "It's a little warm in here."

Theo wanted to laugh, but held back. "Rum has a way of heating up cold nights."

"I love all my children, but Pearl would drive a saint to drink. You already know that."

To that Theo did laugh. "Yes, ma'am, I'm afraid I do."

"She can also drive you mad with her sweetness and caring heart." She glared at Theo. "You're good for Pearl." She patted his hand and stood. "You two are going to be alright."

Theo watched as Sally walked out of the kitchen. He finished his drink then looked around the large empty kitchen. Joe and Sally had raised twelve children in this house. That's the life he wanted. He climbed the stairs then entered Pearl's room. She was lying across the bed snoring. Theo kicked off his shoes, climbed onto the bed and gathered her into his arms.

Pearl circled his waist and held on as she murmured, "I love you, Theo."

He pulled her closer to him. She may not trust him when she was awake, but in her sleep she did.

"Marry me, Theo."

Theo sat up, almost knocking her to the floor. He grabbed her right before she went over the edge of the bed.

"Pearl, wake up."

"I am awake."

He stared at her. "What did you just say?"

Pearl got up then knelt on the side of the bed. She looked up at Theo who was in the bed on his knees looking down at her in disbelief. She understood and prayed it wasn't too late. "I saw that article today and I didn't see me in your life." Tears began to roll down her cheeks. "The thought of you not being here with me is too hard for me to fathom. It's hard for me to express what's inside, but I love you, Theodore Jefferson Prentiss, and there is nothing on God's green earth more important to me than you. Please don't ever wonder about what my decision will be again. For it will always be you." She pulled the blue velvet box from her pocket, opened it and held it up to him. "Our first Christmas together I asked you to wait until I could be a better me. Well, I'm the best Pearl there is because I have you in my life. I have no idea what you got me this year. But baby, all I want for Christmas is you."

Theo's heart shredded at the sight of the tears in her eyes. Until this moment, he'd doubted the depth of her love. He always wondered if he loved her more than she loved him. He reached out and closed the box, then stood on the floor next to her.

Pearl closed her eyes. The rejection in his eyes was too much for her to bear. She wiped the tears from her cheeks.

"Pearl, open your eyes."

She shook her head, too choked up to look at him.

"I need you to look at me."

As hard as it was, she at least owed him the courtesy of her attention when he said what he had to say. She opened her eyes.

The tears shimmering on her lashes, and the sadness in her eyes were too much to take. Theo bent down on one knee, opened the box and gazed into her eyes. "Ms. Pearl Lassiter, will you PLEASEEEEEE, for the third and final time, marry me."

Pearl exhaled so hard she had to catch her breath. She inhaled again, and again, when Theo realized she was hyperventilating. She began waving her hand in front of her face indicating she couldn't breathe. Theo opened the window and looked around. Then he heard her hit the floor.

"You've got to be kidding me."

Epilogue
A Lassiters's Wedding

Six o'clock Christmas morning and the Lassiters' home was a flurry of activities. Six years in the making and the day had finally arrived. Samuel was married to Cynthia and now had two children, Samantha and Franklin. Diamond was married to Zackary Davenport and now had a baby girl, Zoey. And now, Pearl was getting married.

"Who would have ever thought Pearl would get married before me?" Ruby stood at the sink looking out the kitchen window watching the snow fall lightly outside.

"It isn't your time," Sally said as she squeezed her oldest daughter's shoulder.

"I'll be thirty-six years old next month." Ruby washed her hands. "No man and no prospects in sight." She pulled a dishcloth from the rack and dried her hands. "Diamond is married, and now Pearl. Next it will be Opal and Jade and I will be spending another Christmas alone."

Sally wondered why her strong willed daughter was feeling this way. "Ruby." Sally took the towel from her, put it across her shoulder then held her child in her hands. "You are a beautiful woman. Any man is not worthy of you. He has to be someone who is gifted in the art of loving a woman as special as you." Sally held her daughter a moment longer than necessary.

"I love you, Mom. You're good."

Sally laughed and held her daughter at arm's length. "You will do the same for your daughter one day."

"Ha." Ruby took the towel from her mother's

shoulder. "I'll handle the rolls, you get to clean the greens for that lie."

"What lie?" Cynthia asked as she burst through the back door with her arms loaded.

"Nothing important," Ruby replied as she took the box from Cynthia.

"What else do you have?" Sally asked.

"More decorations," Cynthia replied. "We need more hands."

"I'll get the girls." Sally left the room.

"Oh, Ruby, I have something I think you would be interested in." Cynthia pulled off her gloves and reached into her pocket. "My friend Ashley Brooks, she's married to Pearl's old boss James Brooks. Well, a friend of theirs is looking for someone to be the director of some kind of family services agency they are setting up. I know how you like to work with the homeless and thought you might be interested. The only thing is they are looking for someone to start right away. I told them you would call after Christmas." She gave Ruby the card. Ruby slid the card in her pocket as Opal, Jade and Phire ran in the room with pajamas on under their coats and boots on their feet.

"What do you need help with?"

Everyone turned to see Pearl standing behind her mother. Sally jumped into action. "You go back upstairs, young lady. I want to have a word about the dress with you."

"I think it's sexy." Phire walked out the back door.

"You think everything is sexy." Jade walked behind Phire.

"Sexy is in the eye of the beholder," Opal said as four gentlemen in black suits walked in the back door. "Now, that's what you call sexy."

"Opal, let the men in." She turned to see four more men in black behind Samuel. She stepped aside. "This way, guys."

Along with her sisters, they stared as the men walked through the house. "Ho, ho, ho and a Merry Christmas to me," Jade commented.

"Mmm hmm, and amen for the men in black," Ruby added.

"Why are they here?" Jade asked as she watched them move throughout the house.

"President-elect Harrison and his wife are coming to the wedding," Ruby replied.

"What?" Phire huffed. "Man, that means I have to be nice to him. I'm still pissed about what he did to Joshua."

"Girl, he did Joshua a favor." Cynthia put her box on the table. "Can we get the rest of the things from the van? You will have a whole new crop of men to gawk at later."

"Really?" Opal swung around.

"For real?" Phire asked.

"Cool." Jade smiled.

By nine the guys had arrived to move the furniture from the living room and set up chairs for the ceremony. The family room, which had been enlarged a few years ago, was set up with two long dinner tables that sat thirty comfortably. Mathew, Timothy, Adam and Samuel worked diligently getting those tables and chairs positioned just right, they thought. Luke walked in and decided the tables should be arranged in a circle so everyone could face each other. An argument broke out until Theo stepped into the room with Joe.

"Quiet down," Joe said in a very low voice, yet everyone seemed to hear him. "Theo, how do you want the room?"

Luke walked over to him. "You've been waiting for this moment for six years. Make the right decision."

"Or?"

"You'll have to deal with me."

"If you don't get those tables and chairs set up in the next ten minutes every last one of you will have to deal with me." She pointed. "Two long rows, one here and one over there, with a center aisle. One table for two in front of the fireplace," Cynthia yelled from the doorway. Everyone started moving tables and chairs. She turned to Theo. "Where's your mother?"

"She's running a little behind."

Cynthia glared at him. "I'm not taking any mess off of Leonora. If she's not here at six-fifteen I'm starting without her."

Diamond overheard the conversation. She waited until Cynthia was in the kitchen then spoke to Theo. "Is everything okay with your mother?"

"She's had six years to get used to the idea. I'm with Cynthia. If my mother isn't here at the time indicated, we get married without her."

Diamond watched as Theo walked away. The atmosphere did not feel right.

Sally sat in the sunroom watching the children. She laughed as Samantha was bossing her little brother around and he was paying her no mind at all.

"Mom." Diamond entered the room. Her daughter ran to her with her arms raised. Diamond picked her up and kissed her on the cheek. "I think Theo's mother is going to be an issue."

Sally looked sideways at her daughter. "In what way?"

"I don't think she's coming."

Sally stood. "Watch the children."

Diamond watched her mother run out of the room.

"Adam, come with me."

Adam looked at Diamond in the doorway.

"Now, Adam."

"Yes, ma'am." Adam met his mother at the door as the catering staff arrived.

"I wouldn't go out if I were you," Roz, Cynthia's business partner, warned. "They have begun blocking the street off for the President's arrival."

"Mom," Phire called from the top of the stairs. "Pearl is asking for you. She's freaking out. I think she's going to faint...again."

Sally looked up the steps, then out the door and exhaled. "Adam." She took her coat off. "Go to Theo's parents' house. You bring his mother here and I don't care what you have to do to make it happen. You understand me?"

"I'll take care of it." He nodded.

"Do not come back without her."

"Okay." Adam shrugged his shoulders.

Sally approached Pearl's room and could hear her before she reached the door.

"What do you mean, she's not here?"

"It's only noon, Pearl," Opal tried to calm her sister.

"We are supposed to do a walk through at one."

"Theo is here and you're here," Sally said as she walked through the door. "Anyone else is secondary."

"Joshua isn't here," Pearl sighed.

"I know." Sally hugged her daughter. "You know your brother loves you. He's dealing with some demons since that Akande woman." She took Pearl's hands. "But I feel him. His presence is with us." Sally smiled through her sadness about Joshua and the urge to whip Theo's mother's behind. "Joe," she called down the hallway. "Will you ask all the girls to come upstairs and bring a few bottles of champagne?"

"You're getting drunk for the wedding?"

Sally sat down on the bed with the girls. "Of course."

Joe shrugged his shoulders. "Okay."

Adam had just closed the door to his SUV when a man appeared in the backseat.

"Hello, little brother."

The face in the mirror was almost unrecognizable. "Joshua." Adam frowned then smiled. "Mom is going to be ecstatic."

"Where are you headed?"

"I've been ordered to bring Theo's mother to the wedding, willingly or not."

"I'll ride with you."

The passenger door to the vehicle opened. Monique Day, Joshua's trainee, slid inside. "Let's take a ride."

Adam stared at Monique then looked at Joshua through the rearview mirror. "You know I've been approached by the Agency."

"Drive."

An hour later, Sally, Pearl, Ruby, Diamond, Opal, Jade, Phire, and Cynthia were on the bed, the floor, and in chairs all in one room laughing.

"I can't believe you turned the man down three times and he is still around. Now that's love." Cynthia smiled as she downed her fourth glass of champagne.

"Okay, I know about the first and this last one, but when was the second one?" Sally asked.

Pearl, who was on her third glass, sat up against the headboard and laughed. "When Brian was shot."

Cynthia sat up with a gasp. "I remember that. I still cry when I think about it."

"That was a crazy time." Pearl closed her eyes at the memory.

"What happened?" Jade asked.

"Girl, someone shot up JD Harrison's house." Phire sat up in excitement. "Then Brian, who Pearl was sleeping with..."

"You slept with Brian Thompson, the President's body man?" Opal asked, surprised at the news.

"It was before he got married and before Theo," Pearl explained. "And my business." She frowned at Phire.

"Hey, that man was fine, still is even though he is old now."

"I don't care how old he is the man is fineeeeee," Opal huffed.

"Anyway...back to the proposal." Pearl rolled her eyes at Phire. "Theo was his surgeon."

"It was touch and go for days," Cynthia stated. "We didn't know if he was going to make it or not."

"Who shot him?" Jade asked.

"A police officer under order of the Police Chief. See they were trying to take out JD and his family," Phire explained. "But Brian had gotten them out of the house and went back for the little boy. That's when he got shot in the back."

"I missed all of this." Opal shook her head. "So where did the proposal come in?"

"After Brian was released from the hospital, Pearl acted like she was his personal care giver." Cynthia laughed. "She wouldn't let anybody in to see him without going through her first. She spent twenty-four-seven, taking care of him, including baths and things."

"I would have bathed him, too," Phire said. Everyone turned to her in surprise. "What? The man is fine. Theo is nobody's fool."

"I have to agree with Phire on that one, the man is fine," Diamond added. They all looked at her. "I love my Zack, but the truth is the light and Brian Thompson with that face, that body and the way he takes people out. Oh yeah, he's the truth."

"Are you going to let me tell this story?"

"Yes, Pearl, go ahead and tell your story," Sally urged.

"One day Theo came over to check him out. Just to ensure he was not over doing it."

"Theo was checking to make sure *you* weren't over doing it," Sally laughed.

"Hey." The girls gave high fives around the room.

Pearl had to laugh. "You're right on that one, Mommy. He was hot when found me dressing Brian. That's what he pays nurses to do," Pearl imitated Theo. "He was hot about that thing. Anyway, when I went home that night, he asked me about my relationship with Brian." She thought for a moment. "I think that was the first time I knew for sure I loved Theo. He asked if Brian was the reason I wouldn't marry him. I told him no."

"Why did you wait so long to marry Theo?" Ruby asked.

All eyes turned to Pearl. She finished off another glass of champagne and inhaled. "Honestly?" Everyone nodded and the room took on a serious mood. "At first I wanted to establish my career. Theo is a doctor. I did not believe he would stay with me. I thought one day he would find another doctor or lawyer and leave. I wanted to build my career to try to make him proud of me. Then he started talking about having children and I wasn't sure I could do that after what happened in high school. But the most important reason was because I did not want to disappoint all of you again, especially you." She looked at Ruby.

Ruby sat up. "Me?"

"You took care of me every day after I lost the baby. You literally put your life on hold to help me through that time."

"She did that with me too," Diamond added with a smile. "Ruby always made sure I understood my body and how boys looked at me."

"I will never forget when you told me to keep my legs crossed unless I met someone worth having my precious gem." Jade smiled.

Opal sat up. "You told me, love is the ultimate gift you can give a man. Don't give it to anyone who is not worthy of you."

"Ruby didn't tell me any of that," Phire laughed. "She told me I didn't have to worry cause my mouth would keep the boys away."

"True," the other sisters laughed.

Sally smiled as the girls praised Ruby. She glanced at Pearl, who sent her a wink. It was at that moment that Sally knew Pearl's game and realized just how much love her daughter had inside. This was her day, yet she shared this moment with Ruby.

"I wouldn't be marrying Theo today if Ruby hadn't taken the time to help me through the trauma of losing a man and a baby."

Ruby finished her glass, sat it down, then threw a pillow at Pearl.

"Pillow fight," Phire screamed and all the girls jumped in.

"What's going on upstairs?" Theo asked as he sat at the table with the men drinking.

"They are getting drunk and talking about you,"

Joe replied.

"So, what do you suppose Adam is doing to your mother?" Mathew asked.

Theo spit his drink out. "Adam? What are you talking about?"

Samuel gave Mathew a murderous look. "He is helping her do the right thing."

"I have to go get my mother." Theo stood.

Adam appeared in the doorway. "No need."

"What do you mean, no need, Adam? Where is she? Did you hurt her?"

"No, he didn't, but that doesn't mean I won't." Monique appeared from behind him. "Afternoon everyone. Where's Pearl?"

"Upstairs," Luke replied as he stood. "I'll show you."

They reached the room to find feathers from pillows all over the place, in hair, on faces and inside mouths. "What in the hell is going on in here?" Luke asked from the doorway.

"Football," Phire screamed.

All the girls rushed to the door and tackled Luke. Sally and Cynthia sat back and laughed at the scene.

Monique reached down and pulled Pearl from the pile by the back of her sweater. "I need you for a moment." She then looked at Cynthia. "Roz needs you downstairs."

Cynthia squeezed by the pile in the hallway just as Mathew and Timothy came running up the stairs. "It's on now. Let's get out of here."

Pearl was taken out to the gazebo in the back of the yard to find Adam there with Leonora. "You kidnapped Theo's mother?" Pearl rushed over to check on the woman.

"We did not," Adam answered. "She came on her

own accord." He looked down at Leonora. "Isn't that right, Mrs. Prentiss?"

"That's correct."

Pearl frowned, then glanced at Monique.

"Hey, it was not my idea. I came for the wedding."

Then Pearl looked at Adam. "What's wrong with her?"

"Nothing, she's just a little hypnotized."

"You did what!"

"Mother said to get her here and that's what I did."

"Fix her." Adam started to say something. "NOW," Pearl yelled.

"I suggest you two talk first, then I will take her in the house, sit her beside her husband and she will think she came to the wedding with him."

"What are you doing, becoming a mini Joshua?"

"Hey, that's not a bad thing," Monique stated.

"Depends on who you ask."

"Either way," Monique chimed in. "Adam is right. It's best she come to next to her husband. For now you have a unique opportunity to find out why she is so opposed to you."

"I don't want to find out this way."

"Have you found out in the last six years?" Adam asked. Pearl stared at them. "That's what I thought. Take five minutes, ask the question then we'll take her in the house." Adam ran back to the gazebo. "You have to say her name for her to respond." Then he walked back out.

They walked into the yard as Pearl bent down in front of the woman who was about to become her mother-in-law. She did not want to deal with Leonora this way. Pearl only wanted the woman to give her a chance.

"Leonora, I love Theo very much. I am going to be a good wife to him and mother to any children we are blessed with. I will never keep Theo or our children away from you. I want you to be a part of our life." Pearl stood, kissed the woman on her cheek then motioned for Adam to come back in.

"Well?" Adam asked.

"Take her in the house to Edward. And Adam, if you ever do anything like this again I will beat the living crap out of you."

"But Pearl..."

"But nothing. Take her inside."

"All right," Adam huffed. "Leonora, we are going to walk into the house, sit next to Edward and forget everything that happened since noon."

"I need her to remember what I said," Pearl corrected.

"Leonora, I need you to remember your conversation with Pearl." He nodded at Pearl who did not look sure of all of this. "Leonora, I'm going to escort you in the house." He put his arm out as she stood and obediently walked with him inside the house with Pearl following closely behind.

Monique climbed into the SUV parked near the other Agents' vehicles. "Can he do that at will?" Monique asked Joshua.

"Yep." He nodded.

"The Agency could use someone with his talents."

Joshua stared off in the distance. "I don't know if I want this life for my little brother."

"He's a grown man." Monique shrugged. She looked around. "You're not going to say hello to your mother or stay to see your sister get married?"

"Drive."

"I'm just saying, you're here. Say hello. Let them know you're alive."

Joshua looked at the house with the Christmas lights, and all the activity. The things that would give him a sense of family did nothing for him. He did not want his mother to see him this way. "Pull into the alley. We'll stay until the ceremony is over. Just to make sure all goes well."

Monique sighed, "At least that's something," then pulled off.

At five-thirty the guests began to arrive. Theo and his parents were in the living room across from the family room where the ceremony was going to be held.

"Mother, thank you for coming," Theo said as he stood nervously at the entrance, watching people arrive.

"I see a few people from the hospital came, despite the location."

"Leonora," Edward warned. "This is our son's wedding. People are not coming for the location, they are here on Christmas Day, no less, to celebrate in his happiness." Edward tilted his head to encourage his wife to say something positive to their son.

Leonora stood. "Theo." She turned him to face her. "I love you and you know that. I am happy for you," she said as she straightened his bowtie. "I'm not happy with your choice. But I don't have to live with her, you do."

Theo kissed his mother's cheek. It was amazing how alike the two women in his life were. "I love Pearl and I love you. I'm not going to choose between either. I'm going to have both of you in my life. I have a request. For me, will you talk to Pearl?" Leonora took a step back. "Clear the air a little before we take our vows."

"She made you wait six years and you want me to bow to her as well."

"I didn't bow to Pearl, Mother. I waited for the love of my life to figure out I was her knight in shining armor. You know why I waited? You taught me to never settle for less and Pearl is the best. She's told me several times." He and his father laughed and Leonora smiled.

"I bet she has." Leonora gasped. "Edward, your mother is here."

Edward didn't move as Theo and Leonora gazed out the doorway.

"Dad, that is your mother." Theo watched as Brian pointed in their direction.

Jacquelyn Kay Prentiss, in all her elegance, walked into the room. "Good evening."

Edward walked over to his mother whom he had only seen at a distance in years. He kissed her on her cheek. "Thank you for coming."

Leonora rolled her eyes at Edward. "You invited her?"

"I did. Theo, come with me. You don't want to be a witness just in case a murder occurs."

"Theodore." Jacquelyn touched his face. "You are indeed a handsome man. Congratulations. I hope you will be very happy."

Theo, who had only seen pictures of his grandmother, kissed her cheek. "Thank you." He glanced at his mother. "Are you going to be okay?"

"She'll be fine as soon as I finish with her." Jacquelyn closed the door and stared at her daughter-in-law. "Cat has your tongue, Eleanora."

"My name is Leonora."

"I know what your name is." Jacquelyn gave a quick wave of her hand. "Edward asked me to speak with you today in an effort to prevent you from making the same mistake I made. For once in your life be quiet and listen. I told you years ago you were beneath my son and you would make him miserable. I watched as you pulled him down to your level. Over the last thirty-five years I've watched him become the man I always knew he could be. My mistake was I did not recognize you as the woman who could make him that man." She walked over to Leonora. "I'm eighty years old and I've missed the best years of my son's and grandson's lives because of my stubbornness. Don't make the same mistake I did. Embrace your son's wife or take the chance of living a lonely life like I have." Jacquelyn then did something Leonora never thought she would do. She kissed Leonora's forehead then smiled. "Welcome to the Prentiss family." Jacquelyn turned with her long fur coat and gloves on and walked towards the door.

"Jacquelyn," Leonora called out. "You're ninety."

Jacquelyn smiled. "But I look eighty." Then just as gracefully as she'd walked in, she walked out.

Before she could reach the outer door Leonora called out to her. "You should stay for the wedding. It's going to be beautiful. Maybe we can talk afterwards."

Jacquelyn turned back. "I'll stay if you talk with..." She looked at Edward.

"Pearl," Theo offered.

"Very well. Pearl. You talk with Pearl and I'll stay to talk with you."

Edward and Theo watched as Leonora stared up the stairs. "Now?"

"We still have a few minutes before we get started." Theo smiled.

Leonora sighed. "Which room is she in?"

"I'll be happy to show you." Cynthia, who was standing by in case she had to put people out, stepped forward.

Jacquelyn turned to her driver who was on the porch. "I'll be staying with my son and his family for a while."

Cynthia reached the door and knocked. "You have a visitor," she announced as she opened the door then stepped back.

Phire, Opal, Ruby, Diamond, and Jade stepped into the hallway.

"What is she doing up here?" Ruby asked.

"She's here to talk with Pearl," Cynthia replied. "Phire, stay by that door. If anything hops off, you handle it."

"You know I got this." Phire stood outside the door along with the other girls and listened.

"It seems you are going to become my daughter-in-law despite my protests. For my son, I'll accept you as his choice."

"How big of you," Pearl replied as she turned to see Leonora standing in the doorway of her dressing room.

"I don't like you," Leonora stated as she closed the door. "You are selfish and disrespectful. However, I do believe you love my son." She looked around. "If for no other reason than he elevates your status."

"Leonora." Pearl stood to her full height towering over the woman. "Status is important to you. Love is important to us."

"You don't know anything about love," Leonora exploded. "When your family throws you out and disowns you because you dared to love someone outside your race, then you can talk to me about love. If you loved my son, you would have accepted him the way he was when you met him years ago. But no, you have made him into something degrading, by listening to that rap music and putting those damn braids in his hair. I worked my entire life to keep my son away from that and you step in with your hourglass figure and your kinky hair and wiped away the son I raised to be respected. He's a doctor for goodness sake."

The outburst took Pearl by surprise. "Leonora, Theo isn't less of a doctor because he decided to embrace his African-American heritage...your heritage. You have a problem with accepting your natural beauty. That's why you walk around with that not so tight weave. There's nothing wrong with it, but Phire can get one of the girls around the way to make it look like your natural hair." She smiled at the woman. "Listen, Theo loves you. When he looks at me he sees you as that tough woman who fought for the man she loved so many years ago. You apparently were beautiful enough to catch Edward, and your husband isn't a slouch in the looks area. He embraced you as you." Pearl picked up her bouquet. "You might consider giving Edward a peak at the old Leonora. It might spice things up a bit."

"I never want my son to be looked at as a Black man, but as a man. And I certainly don't want my grandbabies going through what I went through all my life."

"Believe me I look at Theo as a man." Pearl grinned. "As for your grandbabies, do you think for one minute I will allow my children to be bullied?" Pearl struck a pose, then took Leonora's arm. "You and I are not going to get along. And that's okay. We are just going to have a love-hate mother-daughter-in-law relationship." She stopped at the door. "However, we are going to make a bond never to put Theo or our children in the middle. Agreed?"

Leonora sighed. "Agreed." She thought for a minute. "You think my hair looks bad?"

"Well, I wouldn't say bad." Pearl shrugged.

"It's whack," Phire said when they opened the door. "But don't worry I'll get She-She to take all that weave out and take you natural. You don't have anything to prove to anybody. Hell, you got your man."

Leonora stared at the young woman. "Pearl, keep her away from me." Then she ran down the stairs.

Sally looked at her daughter. "Theo isn't going to make it to the hotel before he pulls you out of that dress."

"Then I've accomplished my goal. Let's go marry that man."

The Ceremony

The fifty guests were seated theater style to the right in the large family room. The ten-foot Christmas tree was decorated in white and red ornaments with a red bow at the top. Placed next to the tree were seats for Joe and Sally, Edward and Leonora, and a fifth seat was added to accommodate Jacquelyn. The fireplace was decorated with two large, six-stem candleholders with red and white long stem candles. The walkway leading to the fireplace was lined with five chairs on each side decorated in white linen covers with black bows. The staircase leading down into the foyer was garnished with black and white ribbons with red bows at the end of the bannister.

At six-fifteen pm, the lights in the house were dimmed. R&B singer Taylor Brooks began singing

Ribbon in The Sky as the sisters walked in with Ruby leading in black, off the shoulder gowns that showed every curve in their bodies, a single long-stem white rose and a brother dressed in a black tuxedo. The brothers escorted the sisters to their seats, bowed then turned and walked to their seats. At a nod from Cynthia, they all sat. The sisters all crossed their legs pointing towards the fireplace. The brothers rested their foot on their knee all pointed towards the fireplace. The music changed as Pearl began to descend the stairs. All the guests could see was the very bottom of the dress and the three-inch heels on her feet. She turned and met her father at the last step. They could hear Joe's chuckle inside the room.

Joe and his daughter Pearl appeared in the doorway and breathing as Theo knew it ceased to exist. Pearl was his every woman. There was no other like her. The smile on his face intrigued everyone, for other than Theo and her family, no one else had seen her. Pearl was dressed in a white statin tea-strap dress, completely covered in black lace, with a short train behind her. The dress kissed every curve as if it was painted on. A classic single strand of pearls graced her neck with teardrop pearl earrings to match. The back of the dress drew the eyes of every man in the room. Secret Service agents' eyes wandered momentarily from the President-Elect and his wife to the stunning woman walking down the aisle. The most dramatic change was her hair. For her wedding she'd had her hair pressed. It flowed over her shoulders, with soft curls at the end.

"My God, she's beautiful," Jacquelyn whispered.

Leonora had not seen her hair when she was upstairs and she too was shocked.

Pearl stood there next to her father smiling at Theo with tears on the brim of her eyes. "Hi."

Theo reached out to take her hand and Joe slapped it away. "I haven't given her to you yet."

The guests laughed, as Pearl lowered her head and smiled.

The pastor began the service with the traditional wedding ceremony. When he asked if anyone had any objections to the union, all the brothers stood and looked around the room. Joe turned and gave them a look. They all quickly sat back down as the guests laughed. Joe then looked past Pearl to Leonora. She gave a wave of her hand and the Pastor continued as he asked, "Who gives this bride away?" The brothers, sisters, Joe and Sally all said in unison, "We do." Adam added, "And Joshua too." The family all turned to stare at him. Joe placed Pearl's hand in Theo's, then stepped away.

"The couple has written their own vows." He nodded to Pearl.

She gave her bouquet of white roses to Ruby, then took both of Theo's hands. "Theodore Jefferson Prentiss, I love you with all that I am and all that I will be. It is my vow to never take your love for granted. Never to ever let you wonder how much of my heart, body and soul belongs to you. In my heart you come before the President and his one hundred and one speeches. I will not run your mother over with my car, overdraw the bank account or ever wear clothes to bed. Oh, and I will never throw a crowbar at you again. Last, I promise to give you the best Pearl I can be."

The guests were rolling with laughter. A few of the men clapped their hands at the bank account and no clothes to bed.

Once the pastor stopped laughing he looked at Theo. "The ball's in your court, son."

Theo wiped Pearl's tear from her cheek with his thumb, then cleared his throat. "Pearl Ann Lassiter. Thank you for coming into my life. Before you I merely existed. Since the day you came at me with the crowbar, my life was irrevocably changed. The first time I kissed you was to shut you up. Now, it's your voice that puts music in my heart and that dress that started a fire in my loins. I love you with all my heart. You are the very soul of me. I promise not to leave dirty underwear on the bathroom floor. Never to limit the number of shoes you can buy and put a special alarm on the car whenever my mother is approaching, and to give you as many babies as you can handle or die trying." He stepped closer to her. "I promise to strip the doubts and love your fears away. I promise not to ever request any more than you are willing to give, for your love is a precious gift from God that I will treasure for the rest of my life."

The guests wiped at tears as the pastor announced them husband and wife. "You may kiss your bride."

Theo pulled Pearl into his arms then whispered against her lips, "I love you, Mrs. Prentiss."

Pearl wrapped her arms around his neck. "I love you, Dr. Prentiss."

The two kissed as if no one else was in the room and the kiss continued until fireworks exploded in the air. Everyone except Secret Service and JD reacted to the sounds. Cynthia opened the French doors connected to the dining room so all the guests could see the fireworks.

"Joshua," Sally cried out.

They all ran out into the backyard and gathered around the gazebo to watch the array of red, white and blue sparkles beaming against the night sky.

Theo pulled off his jacket and wrapped it around Pearl's shoulders. "What a perfect ending to our day."

Pearl smiled at her husband. "That's what we call a Lassiter Christmas."

The two kissed as fireworks beamed across the sky and snowflakes fell to the ground. The last firework to hit the sky read, Merry Christmas from the Lassiters.